THE JANE WITH
GREEN EYES

THE CLASSIC HANK JANSON

The first original Hank Janson book appeared in 1946, and the last in 1971. However, the classic era on which we are focusing in the Telos reissue series lasted from 1946 to 1953. The following is a checklist of those books, which were subdivided into five main series and a number of 'specials'.

PRE-SERIES BOOKS
When Dames Get Tough (1946)
Scarred Faces (1947)

SERIES ONE
1) This Woman Is Death (1948)
2) Lady, Mind That Corpse (1948)
3) Gun Moll For Hire (1948)
4) No Regrets For Clara (194)
5) Smart Girls Don't Talk (1949)
6) Lilies For My Lovely (1949)
7) Blonde On The Spot (1949)
8) Honey, Take My Gun (1949)
9) Sweetheart, Here's Your Grave (1949)
10) Gunsmoke In Her Eyes (1949)
11) Angel, Shoot To Kill (1949)
12) Slay-Ride For Cutie (1949)

SERIES TWO
13) Sister, Don't Hate Me (1949)
14) Some Look Better Dead (1950)
15) Sweetie, Hold Me Tight (1950)
16) Torment For Trixie (1950)
17) Don't Dare Me, Sugar (1950)
18) The Lady Has A Scar (1950)
19) The Jane With Green Eyes (1950)
20) Lola Brought Her Wreath (1950)
21) Lady, Toll The Bell (1950)
22) The Bride Wore Weeds (1950)
23) Don't Mourn Me Toots (1951)
24) This Dame Dies Soon (1951)

SERIES THREE
25) Baby, Don't Dare Squeal (1951)
26) Death Wore A Petticoat (1951)
27) Hotsy, You'll Be Chilled (1951)

28) It's Always Eve That Weeps (1951)
29) Frails Can Be So Tough (1951)
30) Milady Took The Rap (1951)
31) Women Hate Till Death (1951)
32) Broads Don't Scare Easy (1951)
33) Skirts Bring Me Sorrow (1951)
34) Sadie Don't Cry Now (1952)
35) The Filly Wore A Rod (1952)
36) Kill Her If You Can (1952)

SERIES FOUR
37) Murder (1952)
38) Conflict (1952)
39) Tension (1952)
40) Whiplash (1952)
41) Accused (1952)
42) Killer (1952)
43) Suspense (1952)
44) Pursuit (1953)
45) Vengeance (1953)
46) Torment (1953)
47) Amok (1953)
48) Corruption (1953)

SERIES FIVE
49) Silken Menace (1953)
50) Nyloned Avenger (1953)

SPECIALS
Auctioned (1952)
Persian Pride (1952)
Desert Fury (1953)
One Man In His Time (1953)
Unseen Assassin (1953)
Deadly Mission (1953)

THE JANE WITH GREEN EYES

HANK JANSON

This edition published in 2021 by
Telos Moonrise: Criminal Pursuits
(An imprint of Telos Publishing)
139 Whitstable Road, Canterbury, Kent CT2 8EQ,
United Kingdom.

www.telos.co.uk

ISBN: 978-1-84583-195-0

Telos Publishing Ltd values feedback. Please e-mail any
comments you might have about this book to:
feedback@telos.co.uk

Novel by Stephen D Frances
Cover by Reginald Heade
Silhouette device by Philip Mendoza

First published in England by
S D Frances, July 1950

British Library Cataloguing in Publication Data.
A catalogue record for this book is available from the British
Library.

PUBLISHER'S NOTE

The appeal of the Hank Janson books to a modern readership lies not only in the quality of the storytelling, which is as powerfully compelling today as it was when they were first published, but also in the fascinating insight they afford into the attitudes, customs and morals of the 1940s and 1950s. We have therefore endeavoured to make *The Jane With Green Eyes*, and all our other Hank Janson reissues, as faithful to the original editions as possible. Unlike some other publishers, who when reissuing vintage fiction have been known to edit it to remove aspects that might offend present-day sensibilities, we have left the original narrative absolutely intact – including, in this instance, numerous instances of racial abuse used by some of the deeply unpleasant characters that Hank encounters.

The original editions of these classic Hank Janson titles made quite frequent use of phonetic 'Americanisms' such as 'kinda', 'gotta', 'wanna' and so on. Again, we have left these unchanged in the Telos Publishing reissues, to give readers as genuine as possible a taste of what it was like to read these books when they first came out, even though such devices have since become sorta out of fashion.

The only way in which we have amended the original text has been to correct obvious lapses in spelling, grammar and punctuation, to remedy clear typesetting errors, and in a few instances to substitute American terms for mistakenly-used English ones (such as 'gasoline' in place of 'petrol').

The 'silhouette cover' reissue of The Jane With Green Eyes, *published by New Fiction Press around the end of 1951 or beginning of 1952. To save paper – a particularly valuable commodity in those post-war years – the covers for this edition were overprinted on unused excess copies of those for other Hank Janson titles, mainly – as in the example pictured here –* Milady Took the Rap.

1

It was a Saturday morning with a kinda weekend, holiday atmosphere as I pushed through the swing doors of the Carlton restaurant into the cool shade of the marbled lobby lined with potted ferns and palms.

A large neon sign pointed an arrow toward the bar. There weren't many folks in the bar. I spotted Hal Dean at once, hung my fedora on a convenient hook and strode across to his table.

'It's been a long while, Hank,' he said, shaking my hand vigorously.

He wasn't alone. The dame with him wore a chic little hat with a wisp of a veil. The hat was a kinda screen. When she turned her head ever so slightly I could see only the lower part of her face. She was a quiet, self-possessed, confident type of dame. She watched me coolly and disdainfully, and there was just the merest flicker of interest in her dark eyes when Hal introduced us.

'I'd like you to meet Miss Dewey,' he said. 'Miss Gay Dewey.'

Her manner indicated her boredom as she extended a graceful but languid hand. She was wearing a black fishnet glove on that hand, with delicate open-work as beautiful as a spider's web in the rain. Her fingers were cool and soft in my palm, and when I smiled, her dark eyes seemed to cloud. She withdrew her hand a moment too soon for politeness.

'Sit down, Hank,' said Hal. He snapped his fingers for a

waiter. 'What are ya drinking?'

'Scotch,' I said, without looking at him. I was watching the dame. She turned her head slightly, and the brim of her hat slipped in-between us, like a screen. But not so soon I didn't see the pleased smile fluttering across her lips.

'Hey,' said Hal loudly. 'It was me you came to see. Remember?' He grinned broadly.

I looked sheepish. 'You pick 'em, Hal,' I said. 'You pick 'em good.'

He reached out, and his strong brown hand covered Gay's.

'We're that way, Hank,' he said. 'Anytime now, I'll be signing away my freedom.'

The waiter set a drink down in front of me. I sipped slowly. It was my first drink of the day.

'Well?' said Hal.

'Well?'

'Don't you wanna know why I asked you here?'

'You'll tell me,' I said.

I'd known Hal for many years. He was a lawyer, senior partner in the firm of Dean and Morris. They worked criminal cases, and as a result could sometimes give me inside information. It worked both ways. Lawyers, like everybody, need publicity. If they helped me get a story, I saw their names got mentioned.

Hal Dean wasn't the kinda guy to waste my time. He'd telephoned me that morning saying he had something important. I'd accepted his invitation for a drink without argument. If Hal said it was important, it was important.

'I've got a good lead,' said Hal.

I twirled my glass thoughtfully and shot a sidelong glance at Gay. She'd been watching me. She moved her head casually but quickly, and the brim of the hat slipped down between us again. 'I'm all ears,' I said.

'Wayne's down South defending a nigger,' said Hal. He said it in a despairing kinda way.

'Again!'

He nodded ruefully. 'Again.' He shook his head sorrowfully.

'That boy will never learn sense. He'll never make a living.'

Wayne Morris was Hal's partner, the junior partner. Like so many young, intelligent and sincere men, he was an idealist. He was the champion of the oppressed, always anxious to fight for liberty and justice. You admire a guy like that while you sympathise with him. You admire his courage but you know sometime he's gonna take an awful beating. You can admire a David who bravely faces his Goliath. But when you've knocked around a bit, you know a David conquers a Goliath only once in a coupla thousand years. A modern David faces a tougher opposition when he's up against money, crooked politics and corruption. The modern David takes lots of hard knocks and he learns sense. Then he climbs outta the limelight and slinks around back of Goliath in the shadows, hoping to find Goliath has an Achilles' Heel.

Racial feeling runs high in the States. In the Northern States of America negroes don't fare too badly. But in the South, racial prejudice sometimes mounts to fever pitch. In the South, negroes are deprived of all the rights of citizenship. The only jobs they are allowed to take are inferior, menial jobs. They are forbidden to travel in the same part of the bus as white people and always have to get off the bus to make way for white folks.

There's two kinda laws in the South. One for the white and one for the black. And when a negro has committed an offence, even though it isn't proved, the Southerners sometimes take the law into their own hands and form a lynching party, even on occasions taking the negro from the local jail by force.

A negro who commits an offence is punished unmercifully, especially if that offence is against a white man or woman. But any offence committed against negroes by white people is quickly smoothed over.*

---

* A quotation from the *News Chronicle*, 25 March 1950: 'An all-white jury last night acquitted two white policemen of a charge of beating a negro boy to death. The verdict brought cheers from the public gallery.

'Doyle Mitcham, 24, and James B Clark, 20, were charged with murdering Willie B Carlisle, 18, after he let the air out of their squad car tyres.'

Wayne Morris was the kinda idealistic guy who rushed to defend the victim of injustice. Negroes got short shrift in the law courts. To be arrested was as good as a conviction as far as a negro was concerned. The flimsiest of evidence would be sufficient to condemn a coloured man. That was why Wayne Morris, with his legal training, felt that he was cut out to fight the cause of the coloured people.

'What is it this time?' I asked.

'Usual thing,' said Hal. 'A nigger's been accused of murder. Wayne's been down there since Thursday. The coon hadn't any legal representation until Wayne turned up. Now things are buzzing.'

'How do I fit in?' I asked. 'There's a hundred guys up before the beak every day.'

Hal leaned forward across the table. 'Wayne specially asked me to get in touch with you,' he said. 'He's on to something. He says he can prove the nigger ain't guilty. But that's incidental. He says this is the case of the century. He reckons this is gonna lift the lid right off the South.'

'Don't kill me with suspense,' I growled. 'Give it to me straight.'

Hal grinned and spread his hands. 'That's all I know,' he said. 'Wayne talked to me long-distance. That's all he'd say. Said you were to be there without fail if you wanted the story of a lifetime. He wouldn't give details.'

'How far South?'

'Mississippi,' said Hal.

I grunted. 'What kinda dope am I supposed to be? Travel six hundred miles for a story I don't know the first thing about! I'd be a sap.'

Hal shrugged. 'Take it or leave it,' he said. 'I've just passed on Wayne's message. I guess you don't have to do anything about it. It's up to you.'

'Of all the crazy guys,' I grumbled. I looked up at Hal. 'Can I ring him?'

'Sure you can ring him. But it won't do no good. He won't talk. He won't talk to anybody. He says he's gonna set off a bomb in the court. But he don't risk detonating it until the right moment.'

I looked at Gay appealingly. 'What do you think of a tip-off like that?'

The hat brim shifted a little so I could see one dark eye staring at me levelly. 'It's nice down South, I'm told, this time of the year,' she said softly.

I looked back at Hal appealingly. 'Six hundred miles, fella,' I pleaded. 'That's no joyride.'

He shrugged again. 'It's up to you. I've just passed on the message. Take it or leave it. Want another drink?'

'Sure,' I gloomed.

Hal called the waiter, who replenished our glasses and then glanced at his wristwatch. 'We'll have to be going.'

I looked at him and then looked at the dame. 'Business?'

He chuckled. 'Fishing trip on the lake.'

I looked at the dame and I looked at him. 'Motor launch for the weekend?'

He nodded. 'Uh-huh.'

'Should be nice fishing!'

The dame changed her position and crossed her legs. She was careless with her skirt. Her silk-clad legs were long and slender. She watched me watching her legs, with the suggestion of a smile in her eyes.

'Lucky guy,' I said.

'I think so,' said Hal.

I was imagining her on the deck of a launch, the salt breeze tugging at her hair. I could see her in a white playsuit, the wind pressing the blouse to her body and her long, slender legs glowing gold in the setting sun.

'Can we drop you anywhere?' asked Hal.

'No. Thanks just the same. I'll have to go back to the office.'

I waited until they got a taxi. Gay's fingers were still cool and soft.

'I'll see you around sometime,' I said. I pressed her hand meaningfully, just the tiniest bit.

'Maybe, Mr Janson,' she said. 'Maybe.' Her dark eyes stared

at me full in the face, and the smile still fluttered about her lips.

'Sure, sure, we'll be seeing you,' said Hal heartily. 'Let me know what happens if you decide to take Wayne's tip.' He steered Gay into the taxi, gave| instructions to the driver and waved a farewell.

Somehow, when they had gone, I felt strangely lonely.

I gave the Chief the bare facts just as I'd got them. He ran his fingers through his rumpled hair, rolled his cigar from one corner of his mouth to the other and stared at me thoughtfully with his blue eyes.

'Could be a wild goose chase,' I said.

'Chances are it would be … if anybody else but you went there.'

'What's behind that crack?' I demanded.

He grinned. 'You know the way it is. Every time you go someplace, trouble starts. I ain't saying you cause it, but I reckon you give it a little shove from behind just to help it along.'

'Are you complaining?'

'I ain't complaining,' he said, his eyes twinkling. 'Just commenting.' He looked at the ceiling and screwed up his eyes as he calculated. 'Let me see. Court opens Monday morning, decision probably during the afternoon. You can phone through your report long-distance …' He switched his blue eyes back to me. 'I'll tell you what I'll do, Hank,' he said, in a tone of a fella that's doing a favour. 'I'll hold the front page of the evening edition back for an hour, whatever happens.'

'That's big of you,' I scowled.

'That's okay,' he said magnanimously. 'There's sure to be something else I can splash if I don't hear from you.'

'You want me to go?'

'Sure,' he said. 'Why not? If it's not one thing, it'll be another. You'll get a story.'

'Don't count on it too much,' I said. 'This might turn out to be a waste of time.'

'I'll take a chance,' he grinned.

It was a six-hundred mile run South to Granada, and it was Saturday afternoon. The court didn't open until Monday, which left the weekend intervening. That made me decide to go by car.

I packed a few things in an attaché case, filled up with gas and set off, taking the highway through South Bend into Indiana.

It was an ideal day for driving. The sun was shining – but not too fiercely. The highway was wide and straight. The engine throbbed excitedly, as though thrilled at the prospect of a long run. The miles glided past, smoothly and swiftly, and time passed effortlessly.

I stopped at Egensfield that evening, half my journey completed, and when I set off again on Sunday morning, I knew I had time to spare.

I passed over the State line from Indiana into Kentucky, and just after lunch passed out of Kentucky into Tennessee.

I bypassed the big towns, Jackson and Memphis, and reached the State boundary of Mississippi at the end of the afternoon.

My final destination was Menton. By all accounts it was quite a small town. And I'd been around long enough to know what went on in small towns in the South when a negro was on trial. I decided to stop at Granada that night and drive into Menton early on Monday morning.

It was a wise decision. I'd never have found lodgings overnight in Menton. Even in Granada, lots of folks were stopping overnight on their way out to Menton.

You'd have thought there was a carnival in Granada. Cars thronged the car parks outside the hotels, and the bars were crammed. There was only one topic of conversation. The trial. And while they talked about the trial, you sensed they were really interested in something deeper. There was a kinda undercurrent everywhere, an unspoken question. Everybody wanted to know the answer to that question. Everybody was going to Menton to find out the answer. But nobody dared ask the question. Yet it was there all the time, hovering on the air, lurking at the back of folk's eyes, written in the lines of their faces and motivating their methodical preparations for an early-morning departure for Menton.

The question was crystal clear. But nobody dared to voice it. Nobody had the courage to ask out loud: *Is there going to be a lynching?*

2

I got up extra early. Even so, I was part of a procession. There was a line of cars in front of me as far as I could see, and another long chain stretching behind.

I got an uneasy feeling. I began to wish I hadn't come. I didn't want to be adding my support to this one-way traffic into Menton.

I couldn't understand it. I'd seen a lotta these folks in Granada. Many of them had been stopping in my hotel. I'd drunk at the bar with them, talked to them. They'd been ordinary folks. A newly-married insurance agent with his young wife; a stockbroker; a farmer; a real estate agent: all ordinary, decent folks. I'd stood there in the bar listening to them. They seemed ordinary folks in all respects except one. They had a blind spot. They talked about negroes as though they weren't human beings. They called them 'niggers', 'coons', 'darkies' and 'black trash'.

One fella told me, 'Niggers are made different.' He said coloured folk don't feel pain like white people. They have to be hit harder to feel as badly hurt.

It got my head in a whirl. If it had been just one guy, I'd have thought he had an obsession. But it wasn't one guy. It was lots of folk. Moreover, they were ordinary, decent folk. And the way they talked about negroes as though they were talking about animals was so natural I began to wonder if it was me that had the blind spot instead of them.

It was a gala day for Menton. Before we ran into town, police patrols and white-coated attendants were guiding the cars off the road into fields converted into emergency parking lots. Although it was early in the morning, there'd been lots of folk before me. The parking lots were jammed with cars, long, neat rows of cars, all types, from glossy limousines to battered old wrecks.

I parked my car where directed, locked it and mingled in the crowds sauntering into Menton with the chattering light-heartedness of a holiday crowd.

But the holiday crowd atmosphere changed suddenly and dramatically as we got into Menton. It wasn't far along the road – maybe a hundred yards. A kinda hushed, awed silence overcame everyone.

Menton wasn't even a town. It was just a name on the maps, and not on many maps at that. There was a long, wide main street opening out into a kinda square, with a few houses and streets leading off the Main Street.

The Main Street was the shopping centre. There was a grocery stores a clothiers, a drug store, a barber's shop, the inevitable bank, and a hardware store.

But all the shops were closed. The proprietors stood in their shirtsleeves on the boardwalks outside their shuttered windows. And the dusty highway was jammed with sullen, silent, waiting men and women. There was a kinda hushed expectancy over everyone that made them talk in whispers. There was the tense atmosphere of a crowd that is waiting for something to happen. And as more and more folk thronged into the Main Street, others shifted, made way for them, and the newcomers stood there like the others, waiting expectantly for what was to happen.

The crowd had congregated where the Main Street widened out into a carpark. But it was at this point that the local jail was situated. It was only a small town. That was why the council offices, jail and court were all in the same building.

It was a grim, brick-built two-storey building. Wide steps led to the front door, and a coupla well-built fellas with rifles under their arms lounged on either side of the doorway. They both wore Deputy stars on their hickory shirts.

There was no mob panic. They just stood and waited. There was no shouting, no sudden surging forward toward the jail. They just stood there, tensed, waiting. Somehow, that seemed to make it all the more ominous. The crowd was relentless, willing to wait forever if necessary.

I shouldered my way through toward the jail. I thrust past hard-handed farmers, slickly dressed city men, lightly-dressed women and groups of youths. Nobody resented me. But everybody watched me.

I got to the foot of the steps, and one of the Deputies took his cigarette from between his lips and moved his rifle gently so that it came up level with my knees.

'I shouldn't come any further, fella,' he advised quietly. His grey eyes stared at me impassively.

I looked at him, I looked at his gun and then I looked back into his eyes again. 'I'm a reporter,' I said.

'Court opens hour and a half,' he said mechanically. 'There'll be an inspection of credentials then. No-one allowed in before.'

That was fair enough. I turned away, leaned against some fencing and pulled out my cigarettes. Folk were still arriving. The crowds were getting dense. As I glanced around, I could see lots of local folk had got their shotguns with them. Here and there I caught a glimpse of a significant bulge weighing down a coat pocket or bulking through a windjammer. I looked back at the two Deputies and suddenly realised they wouldn't be able to stop this mob if they made up their minds to try it.

The sun was coming up now, and the shifting of a thousand feet was sending particles of dust floating in an invisible cloud. I took off my jacket and draped it over my arm. I loosened my tie and unbuttoned my shirt. The middle-aged guy next to me, wearing a black leather coat and blue jeans, grunted and took off his coat. His shirt was dirty, and a great sweat-patch circled his armpits. I could even smell him. Heavy and sweaty, like an over-worked horse. He took a handmade cigarette from the corner of his mouth and grunted: 'Waste of time.'

'Yeah,' I said, noncommittally.

'Get it settled,' he said. 'Silly. Wasting all this time.'

I grunted. The voice of the crowd was a low murmur. A low, ominous murmur. It was like the distant sound of an angry surf beating upon the beach. Like the sea, it was relentless and determined.

'Could have been all settled by now,' grunted the fella with the sweat-patches.

'Sure could.' I didn't trust myself to say too much. This crowd was dynamite. It needed just a spark to set it off.

The man spat. 'Ought to go in there and get him out,' he grunted. 'Plenty of gasoline. Gasoline don't cost much.'

'That's right,' I said. I was clenching my fists tightly.

'Why don't they get him out?' he growled. 'String him up. Set him alight. Waste of time waiting here.'

I knew now what they were waiting for. They were waiting for each other. Everyone was waiting for somebody else to make the first move. That was the key to this grim, ugly, waiting silence. They'd come to see a lynching. And when it started they'd take their part. They'd stand and watch and shout and encourage. Some of them would splash gasoline over the writhing, tortured body, others would apply the matches, light torches, parade and shout and behave like beasts. There would be many hands ready to pull on the rope. There would be many fists to hammer, punch and gouge. But …

The crowd was a coward. It was waiting for a lead. It was waiting for the first man to lead the way.

It needed one individual to make the first move. Everything afterwards would be automatic. From then onwards he would not be an individual, he would be part of an angry, howling mob.

The man with the sweat-patches ground out his finished cigarette and began making another. There were beads of sweat on his forehead, and he shifted uneasily from one leg to another. He was getting tired.

'Waste of time,' he grumbled. 'What are we waiting for?'

'Waiting for the trial,' I suggested. 'Waiting to see if he's guilty.'

He spat. 'He's guilty. A no-good nigger. That's what he is.' He spat again.

'Never can tell,' I said. 'Could be he's proved innocent.'

He stared at me, and his face grimaced with disgust. He eyed me with loathing and spat again, slowly and deliberately. His brown, tobacco-stained spittle hit the dust an inch from my shoe. The atmosphere was tense, a faint spark could start the conflagration. Any triviality could detonate the explosive, slumbering hatred of this waiting mob. I clenched my hands more tightly and forced myself to grin weakly.

'I guess you got me wrong, fella,' I said weakly.

'Yeah?' he said, curling his lips. He eyed me expectantly, hoping I'd add something. I kept my mouth shut. He cleared his throat and turned his eyes away toward the jail. He stood there, shifting from one foot to the other, watching, waiting.

Ten minutes before the court was due to open, a broad-shouldered guy wearing a Stetson, riding breeches and a whipcord jacket posted himself at the foot of the steps.

He was wearing a Sam Browne belt with an unbuttoned holster so that he could get at his revolver quickly. His Sheriff's badge glinted brightly in the morning sun.

The crowd was silent, like an invisible enemy waiting to pounce. They watched him wordlessly as he took up his position with legs astride, face hard and expressionless and hands hanging limply at his sides, near his revolver.

Shortly afterwards, a tall, angular, white-haired guy dressed in black shouldered his way through the crowd. There were a coupla of other guys with him. The Sheriff stood on one side so they could pass, and he nodded and said, 'Morning, judge.'

You could hear the whisper rippling over the sea of faces like the ripples from a stone dropped in the centre of a quiet pool.

'It's the judge. The judge has arrived.'

And then Wayne Morris arrived. He had an assistant with him. Wayne was hard-faced, tight-lipped. He looked neither to left nor to right as he pushed his way through toward the jail.

I worked my way across to him, and when he was at the foot of the steps: 'Hiyah, Wayne,' I said quietly.

He looked up quickly, startled. Then his face softened. 'Hiyah, Hank,' he said quietly. 'Come on in, will ya?'

The Sheriff stood squarely across the path. His face was hard, granite-like, and his eyes were blue, like ice.

'Who's this guy?' he demanded.

I sensed Wayne kinda tighten up inside. 'He's a friend of mine,' he said. 'A reporter.'

'We got reporters,' said the Sheriff.

'This one's from Chicago. The *Chicago Chronicle*.'

'We got reporters,' repeated the Sheriff, obstinately.

Wayne breathed hard. He spoke in a low tone, so that the crowds around wouldn't hear. 'I've had about as much opposition as I can take, Sheriff. I know you hate my guts for taking this case. But I'm warning you, Sheriff, if you don't let this reporter through, I'll raise all hell. I'll ask for an adjournment pending enquiries into the muzzling of the press. I'll see Senator Mason personally, myself, and I'll get the Feds down here so quick ...'

'Okay, okay,' said the Sheriff, surlily. His blue eyes glinted at me and he spat tobacco juice from the corner of his mouth. He wiped the back of his hand across his lips and then reluctantly stepped to one side.

'Just follow your nose,' Wayne told me.

The court was a large room containing moveable wooden benches. The judge's bench was a large table on a raised dais. You got the impression right away that Menton didn't have much lawlessness; not the type that required a regular court sitting, anyway.

Wayne took me down front of the court and gave me a seat at his table. Then he excused himself on account he had to see his client, and went out through a side door.

I was the only guy in the courtroom apart from a tobacco-chewing janitor, who was sweeping the floor in a desultory manner.

I got up and crossed over to the window. The crowd was

still there. It was staring at the courthouse now with the steady, unblinking gaze of a basilisk. All those folk out there, just waiting, staring, sent a cold shudder running down my spine. They weren't human. There was an emotionlessness about them beyond any experience I'd ever had. There were a thousand eyes watching that courthouse, but each pair of eyes had a different brain behind them. A thousand different brains, thinking, hating and broodingly waiting. And with a strange soundlessness, like a black, silent pool of unplumbed depths.

The Sheriff was allowing other folk to come in now. Each had a paper that he checked. I guessed they were the jury, and my guess was confirmed when a Deputy ushered twelve of them onto one bench.

They were all men and they were all white. Furthermore, they were all local citizens. They were farmers, herders and storekeepers. The butcher was there with his apron, his shirtsleeves rolled up over his fat arms and his apron smirched with fresh blood. The jurors didn't talk among themselves. Mostly they stared at me. It was pretty plain they'd made up their minds about the case already. I was different. They hadn't made up their minds about me.

For the first time, I saw movement from the waiting crowd outside. The Sheriff was letting in the public now. Those people nearest the doorway were elbowing their way up the steps. The Sheriff and his Deputies were having their work cut out coping with them, but they managed, and no man wearing a gun was allowed into the courtroom.

The court filled up quickly. They flooded the place. A dozen squeezed onto a bench meant to hold six, and when the benches were full they sat in the aisles and leaned against the walls. They were standing at the back, packed like sardines, and when the Sheriff closed the courtroom door he looked like a subway guard trying to compress his passengers into an already over-full compartment.

I couldn't get rid of that uneasy feeling. There was an atmosphere about the place. An atmosphere provided by the public. A relentless, ominous atmosphere. Nobody spoke.

Nobody laughed. They just waited. Waited!

Wayne and his assistant joined me at the table. I was thankful to be at his table. It gave me leg room and arm room, and the sun was higher now, beating on the roof with fierce intensity. Already the heavy, sweaty odour of feet, bad breath and perspiration was clogging the air. Wayne, with his stiff white collar and newly-laundered shirt, was the only man in the courtroom who looked cool.

'This gonna take long?' I asked.

'Not long, I hope.' He unzipped his briefcase and took out a sheaf of papers. The frown of concentration on his face was a clear request not to bother him.

Level with our table on the other side of the room were three other guys. They, too, had papers and pens ready, and official looking files and documents. A scraggy-looking guy with an old-fashioned tie loosely tied around his neck was obviously the DA. He wore a pair of metal-rimmed glasses that had been clumsily repaired with twine, and his grey pants flapped baggily around his long, thin, angular legs.

I hung my jacket on the back of my chair, loosened my tie some more, untied my shoelaces and fanned myself with a newspaper. The fanning didn't get me any cooler. It just proved that the thick stench of sweating bodies was getting even thicker.

The side door opened and one of the Deputies yelled that the judge was about to enter.

Nobody got up when the judge came in, and he didn't seem to expect them to get up. The first thing he did was to hang his jacket on the back of his chair and mop his face with a large red handkerchief. He glared around the court and then said testily: 'Let's get this durned case settled. It's gonna be stinking hot.'

They brought in the defendant then. The Sheriff knew what he was doing. He had a coupla armed Deputies standing just in front of the public, and two other Deputies escorted the negro to a chair by the side of the entrance. What was unnerving was the way the crowd didn't react. There were no cat-calls, no jeers, no snarls of disapproval. Only a slight rustling as heads craned to see him better. That was all. Then the ominous silence and the atmosphere of patient waiting. It was as though the crowd were looking at a man already dead. I guess maybe that's how they thought about him.

I guess maybe that's how Joe Robson thought about himself.

He was a young fella, maybe 30, broad-shouldered and powerfully built. He was wearing a pair of blue jeans several sizes too small, which were stretched tightly across his sturdy thighs. His white singlet was grimy and torn. He gave one wild, apprehensive glance around the court and then sat with his face buried in his hands. You could see right away that Joe Robson hadn't any illusions about the outcome of this case.

The judge said loudly: 'If we get this case wiped off snappy, we all kin get outta this oven.' He mopped his face again with the red handkerchief.

The DA got to his feet slowly, cast Wayne a sneering look and then turned back to the judge. 'I ain't reckonin' on taking long, George,' he said slowly. 'But some folks thet cum aroun' here poking their long noses into ...'

Wayne was on his feet. 'Objection,' he yelled.

'See whad I mean, George?' said the DA.

'Objection,' said Wayne again.

The judge sighed wearily. 'Objection sustained,' he said. Then he looked at the DA apologetically. 'Cut out the frills, Al,' he said. 'Jus' keep tuh the point. We doan't want blasted Northerners saying we all doan know how to run our courts.'

Wayne sat down, and the first witness took the stand. He was a rugged-faced guy with shifty grey eyes and one eyebrow that was a good inch higher than the other. He took the oath and then settled himself comfortably, awaiting the DA's questions.

'Your name?'

'Lew Kirk.'

'Yuh are a relative of the deceased, Arthur Kirk?'

'I'm his cousin.'

'Will yuh tell the court, in your own words, what happened on the night of the tenth?'

Lew settled himself more comfortably in his chair, licked his lips and wiped his sweaty hands on his handkerchief. Then he leaned forward and spoke slowly and carefully, as though weighing every word. I was fascinated by the way his raised eyebrow moved up and down.

'Art was my cousin, see. We worked together. Lawyers. I guess we got along all right. We shared the same house. He had the top half and I had the bottom. I guess if I'd known that durn nigger was gonna ...'

'Confine yourself, please,' said the DA. 'What happened on the night of the tenth?'

Lew shot Robson a look of hatred and then said loudly, as though talking to the crowd: 'I had an appointment in Granada.' He smirked. 'It was a special appointment. I won't give full details. A lady was involved.'

'That is for the court to decide,' said the judge ponderously.

Lew's face lost its smirk. 'I guess I'd kinda like to leave that bit out, judge, if it's okay. It don't affect the evidence no way.'

'Carry on,' said the DA. 'We'll come back to that if necessary.'

Lew gulped and carried on. 'I left Menton about eight o'clock, I guess. I stayed all night in Granada and came back early the next morning. I could see right away something was wrong, on account the light was still burning. I went into Art's study and there he was, stretched out on the floor with a gun in his hand. I didn't even have to get close to him. I could tell right away that he was ... dead.'

The DA had picked up a shining object from his desk; he showed it to Lew. 'Is this the gun?'

Lew looked at him and then at the gun and nodded. 'Sure,' he said. 'That's the gun. I'd know it anywhere, it's Art's own gun.'

'And what did you do when you discovered this ...?'

'It kinda stunned me,' said Lew. 'Art was my cousin, and seeing him dead like that ...'

'What practical things did you do?' persisted the DA. He was feeling the heat himself now. He didn't want to waste a single moment.

'I telephoned,' said Lew. 'I telephoned the Sheriff. He come right on over with his Deputies. I left everything just the way it was.'

'I want you to think very carefully now. When you first saw your cousin lying dead, in which hand was he holding the revolver?'

Lew answered so quickly it was obvious he had been rehearsed many times. 'He was holding the gun in his left hand.'

'Do you find anything surprising in that?'

'I sure do,' said Lew loudly. 'My cousin was right-handed.'

'Almost as though the gun had been put in his hand after he'd been shot,' said the DA gently.

Wayne was on his feet. 'Objection,' he yelled.

The DA grinned. The judge grinned. 'Objection sustained.' He smiled at the Jury. 'You'll put out of your minds the comment just made by the DA.' The Jury appreciated the point. They grinned, too.

Wayne sat down, muttering angrily to himself, and his white face showed two red spots burning angrily high up on his cheeks. I didn't know much about court procedure, but I could see Wayne was up against it.

The DA cleared his throat and pointed at Robson. 'Do you recognise the defendant?'

'Look up,' said the judge.

Robson still had his face buried in his hands.

'Look up,' repeated the judge.

One of the Deputies seized hold of Robson's kinked hair and jerked his head back. His face came up out of his hands, and the whites of his eyes rolled despairingly.

'Sure I know him,' said Lew. 'Used to be our gardener. No-good trash, that's what he is.'

'Why no-good?' asked the DA gently.

'A lazy good-for-nothing,' said Lew. 'Always stealing vegetables and fruit. Arthur gave him the push. Bundled him out, neck and crop, just two weeks before he died.'

'And did Robson object to that?'

Lew frowned. 'I'll say he did. I heard him talking to himself. He didn't know I was around. He was talking to himself like these fellas do. He was saying he was gonna kill Arthur. Shouting out how he was going to kill him, whip him to pieces.'

'You actually heard these words yourself?'

'Those very words,' said Lew. 'Talking to himself, he was, just down by his shack. He was holding a bamboo cane and lashing at a tree-trunk. He kept saying, "That's for you, Arthur Kirk, and that, and that. I'll kill you, that's what I'll do. I'll kill you!"'

'Talking to himself that way,' said the DA, 'would you say that he was crazy?'

'He wasn't crazy,' said Lew, viciously. 'He was mad at being sacked. As angry as hell, and when he looked around and saw me, he dropped the cane and ran as fast as his feet would carry him.'

'And how far is Robson's shack from your house?'

'About a hundred and fifty yards. There's a path through the woods that leads straight to his shack. Working around the place so much, I guess he just naturally trod that path himself.'

The DA picked up two heavy silver candlesticks from his bench and held them up so that Lew and the rest of the court could see them clearly. 'These are exhibits two and three,' he said. 'Can you identify these, Mr Kirk?'

Kirk nodded. 'Those belonged to my cousin,' he said. 'He always had them in his study. He was very fond of them.'

'And were you surprised when the Sheriff found these two candlesticks in Robson's shack?'

Lew looked at the candlesticks, then he turned and looked at Robson's bowed head. 'Normally I mighta been,' he said. 'But seeing the way things were, with Arthur lying dead, I guess I weren't surprised.'

The DA hitched his baggy trousers around his thin legs and grinned at Wayne. 'Your witness,' he said, and sat down.

Wayne got up slowly, with a tiny frown tugging at his forehead. He went across and stood staring down at Lew. He didn't say anything. He just stared. Lew grinned back at him, but the grin quickly slipped from his face. His features straightened themselves out. A few moments later his raised eyebrow began to twitch nervously.

'These candlesticks,' said Wayne. 'When did you last see them in your house?'

'They were always there,' said Lew. 'Up until the time Robson killed Arthur, that is.'

'Answer my question,' snapped Wayne. 'You're giving evidence now. Evidence of facts. I'm not interested in your private opinion. Who killed your cousin has yet to be proved. When did you last see these candlesticks?'

'The same day I went to Granada, I guess. The day before my cousin was killed.'

'You're sure of that?'

'Sure I'm sure.'

'And will you tell the court how you are sure? Will you tell the court exactly why you particularly noticed those candlesticks on the day you went to Granada?'

Lew spread his palms. 'Well, I guess I didn't have no particular reason to notice them. I guess I just did.'

'Do you mean that you guess you saw them?'

'I guess I just did see them.'

'The question is,' said Wayne slowly, 'whether you guess rightly or wrongly. We are concerned with facts. Are you positive you saw those candlesticks that day, and if so, what makes you so positive?'

Lew looked confused. 'I reckon I musta done,' he said.

Wayne bored in, his voice suddenly hard. 'Are you sure your cousin Arthur didn't give those candlesticks to Robson? Are you sure that Robson hadn't had those candlesticks for at least two weeks before your cousin was killed?'

'Why should my cousin give a loafing good-for-nothing nigger a pair of candlesticks?'

'I'm coming to that,' said Wayne. 'Didn't your cousin Arthur give those candlesticks to Robson to keep him quiet?'

Lew's face went a shade paler. He licked his lips nervously

and his eyebrow twitched rapidly. 'I don't know what you're talking about,' he blustered.

Wayne said slowly and loudly, 'Is it not a fact that a week before Robson was sacked, you and your cousin beat him so savagely that he was unable to work? Is it not a fact that when you realised you had gone too far, you gave him the candlesticks and told him to keep his mouth shut?'

'Objection,' roared the DA. He was up on his feet, with his long scraggy arms stretching toward the judge. 'Witness is not on trial and cannot be made to give evidence against himself.'

Wayne protested to the judge. 'This evidence is vital to the case on hand.'

The judge grinned at him openly. 'Objection sustained,' he said.

I thought Wayne was going to burst a blood-vessel. He got himself under control somehow and turned back to Lew.

'I suggest that you and your cousin gave those candlesticks to Robson to keep his mouth shut about the two of you beating him within an inch of his life.'

The DA was on his feet again. 'Objection,' he yelled.

The judge's gavel thumped the table. 'Objection sustained,' he roared.

There was a glitter in Wayne's eyes as he turned back to Lew.

'I suggest that you and your cousin gave those candlesticks to Robson ...'

The judge's gavel interrupted. Wayne looked at the judge. The judge said slowly: 'Jest try that once more, Mr Wayne. I'm in charge of this hyar court. I've ruled yuh out of order. One more flagrant violation of my jurisdiction and I'll have you removed from the court.'

If Wayne had been a shooting man I guess he'd have been shooting all over the place. He stood there tensed, with his hands gripped at his sides for maybe fully half-a-minute, before he spun on his heels and walked back to his table.

The judge grinned, the DA grinned, and Lew grinned broadly at the crowded court.

I leaned across and whispered in Wayne's ear, 'You're beating your head against a wall, fella.'

He was breathing hard. Anger was simmering inside him, almost at boiling point. 'I'll get them yet,' he said. 'They've got a surprise coming.'

The next witness was a local ballistics expert. He identified the bullet found in the murdered man as being fired by the gun in the murdered man's hand. Wayne had no questions to ask him, and no questions to ask the doctor who gave evidence that Arthur Kirk had died by reason of a bullet in his heart.

Then came the fingerprint expert. He didn't look very expert to me. He sounded like he knew his part off by heart. All his questions he answered pat.

'Have you identified the fingerprints found on the gun?'

'Yeah. They were the fingerprints of Mr Arthur Kirk.'

'Were there any peculiar features about those fingerprints?'

'Yes, sir, there sure was. They didn't appear on that gun natural. Those prints were blurred. You get that kinda blurred effect when you press a gun into a man's hand and try to pretend he was holding the gun.'

'In your opinion,' said the DA slowly, 'the gun was pushed into Art Kirk's hand after he had been shot?'

'That sure is my opinion.'

Wayne shrugged. 'Absolute violation of court procedure,' he muttered. 'Leading questions all the time.'

'Didn't you expect that?'

He nodded glumly.

The DA was looking at Wayne from the corner of his eyes as though almost expecting him to interrupt him. 'Were you at the scene of the crime?'

'The Sheriff called me in soon after he had got there.'

'Did you notice any other peculiar features?'

'I sure did,' said the man. 'Powder-burns. Now, if a guy ups and shoots himself, he holds the gun close. That means he's gonna get powder-burns on his hands and on his clothes.' He shook his head. 'There weren't no powder-burns on Art Kirk. Whoever shot him musta been at least six feet away.'

'Very interesting,' said the DA, nodding his head and looking at the jury, making sure they'd heard this.

'Another funny thing, too,' said the witness. 'When a guy's gonna shoot himself, he don't shoot himself in the heart. No siree. He puts the gun to his temple, where he's sure he won't miss. I never bumped up against a case of a man shooting himself through the heart.'

'Your witness,' said the DA, grinning.

Wayne crossed to the witness, and somehow he seemed quite tired. 'Are you a good democrat?' he asked.

'I sure guess I am,' said the man. 'I'm an American, through and through.'

Wayne said softly. 'Would you call a negro "Mister"?'

'What! Call a nigger "Mister". I'd be doggorn, suh.'

'In short,' said Wayne smoothly, 'you have a racial prejudice.'

The DA coughed loudly, and the witness caught his eye. He smiled broadly. 'I ain't got racial discriminations,' he said. 'I'm a democrat. But when it comes to niggers, well, I guess they just ain't humans.'

Wayne sighed loudly. 'All right,' he said quietly. 'You can get down.'

When Wayne sat down, I asked, 'Just what are they getting at?'

'It's clear enough. First they're proving that Arthur Kirk didn't shoot himself; then they're proving that Robson had a row with and a grudge against Arthur Kirk; then they're proving he had the candlesticks; and there you are. Robson killed Arthur Kirk in order to get the candlesticks.'

'That's crazy,' I said. 'That's hardly any evidence at all.'

'That's all the evidence required, down here,' he said bitterly. 'Look at that jury. They don't want any evidence at all. They're just burning for an opportunity to give a guilty decision.'

'They need law in these parts,' I said.

'They sure do,' he agreed. 'The court case is only a formality. I guess it squares their conscience. Sometimes there's enquiries after a lynching, and sometimes it gets awkward if they don't have a verdict of guilty before the lynching takes place.'

The DA was facing the jury now. There were trickles of perspiration on his thin, scrawny neck. He said: 'I guess that kinda closes the case for the prosecution, folks. You can see the way it is. That derned nigger is as guilty as hell. But the law's gotta be obeyed. I guess we just gotta sit here in this stinking hothouse a little longer, listening to our city friend saying his piece awhile before we give a verdict.' He looked at the judge. 'I guess that's all for my side of it, George.'

The judge mopped his face with his handkerchief. Then he scowled at Wayne. 'I guess we ain't got all day, Mr Morris,' he said. 'If you're taking up the court's time much longer, we're gonna be reduced to grease-spots.'

Wayne stood up and stared at the judge levelly. 'I won't take much time, your honour,' he said, sincerely. 'I just intend to prove beyond a shadow of doubt that Robson could not have committed this crime. That won't take long.' His eyes roved across to the jury. 'Even though the jury may find it difficult to reconcile their desires with the decision they will be forced to make.'

The jury grinned at him. They'd made up their minds. They just couldn't see how Wayne was gonna make them change their minds.

'I wish the defendant to take the stand,' said Wayne.

There was that same silent, ominous craning of necks. They were looking at a dead man, watching every movement he made, the despair in his bowed shoulders and the dread of what was to come that showed in his eyes.

Robson sat there, hunched, his head lowered and his eyes fixed on the floor. His attitude suggested he was expecting things to be thrown at him at any moment.

Wayne stood in front of him, cutting the crowds off to give him confidence. 'Sit up straight, Joe,' he said.

Joe rested his hands on his knees and then slowly straightened up. But he still kept his eyes lowered, fixed on the waistline of Wayne's trousers.

'Don't worry, Joe,' said Wayne. 'Everything's going to be all right. Just concentrate on the questions I'm going to ask you. Don't be afraid.'

The judge rapped with his gavel. 'Mr Wayne Morris,' he pleaded. 'This ain't a kindergarten. We're here to hear evidence.'

Wayne licked his lips and glared at the judge. Then he turned back to Robson. 'Where were you that night?' he asked quietly.

Joe didn't answer.

'You must answer, Joe,' he urged. 'Where were you that night? What were you doing?'

Joe said in a low, tremulous voice, 'I was in my shack, suh. I was there all night.'

'You didn't go to Arthur Kirk's house and you didn't shoot him?'

'Ah did not,' said Joe loudly. He seemed to get strength from somewhere. He denied it not as though he was trying to convince the court, but as though his own dignity had been affronted. 'May de good Lord have me burned in everlasting fire if I killed anyone, suh.'

Wayne still spoke quietly, almost persuasively. 'I don't want you to be afraid, Joe. I want you to be truthful. I want you to tell me exactly where you got those candlesticks.'

'Ah got them from Mr Kirk. He dun give me those. He dun said I was a good boy. He give me them himself. I so proud of them.'

The silence in the court was like a blanket. So was the stench of sweating bodies. The sun was beating down on the wooden roof and cooking the sour air inside.

'Did Mr Kirk say he was giving you these candlesticks for any reason? Any reason at all?'

'Yes, suh,' said Joe. 'Yes, suh, he sure did.' His eyes rolled.

'Try to remember his exact words,' said Wayne gently.

'Ah remember his exact words, suh. Masser Kirk, he said "Them candlesticks are a present for you, boy, on account of you doan't make no trouble for me about that larruping I gives you."'

There was a kinda hiss around the court. It was as if everybody breathed out at the same time. Joe knew what it meant. He kinda cowered in his seat. Publicly he had accused a white man of committing an offence against him. That was a thing most negroes were never foolish enough to do. They'd learnt by bitter experience that the white man has more ways than one of paying back.

'What else did he say?' asked Wayne.

Joe shook his head and clenched his lips together. His eyes were mutely appealing. It was almost as though he was saying: *Let's get it over with. I don't wanna cause no more trouble.*

Wayne sensed Robson's resistance. He stood back a pace and said, 'Stand up, Robson.'

Robson stared at him, surprised.

'Stand up,' rapped Wayne in a commanding voice, and like a horse that has heard the crack of a whip, Robson slowly pulled himself to his feet. He stood there limply, his hands hanging at his sides.

'Turn around,' said Wayne.

Joe's face gaped at him blankly.

'Turn around,' almost shouted Wayne.

Joe didn't understand what it was about. But he understood the order. He turned slowly. He stood there with bowed shoulders, his black skin gleaming with perspiration.

Wayne stepped forward, took the grimy, worn singlet between his hands and ripped it down the back. Joe still stood there, surprised but obedient. His singlet hung down, revealing for all the court to see the scarred wheals crisscrossing his black skin.

Wayne turned Joe so that his back was to the jury. There was an angry glitter in Wayne's eyes. 'Look at that, you men,' he said. 'Look at it, stare at it, and remember that this inhumanity is the work of a white man, the work of Arthur Kirk.'

'Objection,' yelled the DA. He was on his feet, waving at the judge.

'Objection sustained.'

Wayne laughed bitterly. It sounded strangely clear in that stuffy, broiling courtroom.

'Objection sustained, your honour,' he said sarcastically. 'So was the beating.'

The judge blew his nose loudly.

Wayne led Joe back to the chair beside me, and the judge mopped his face and peered at him.

'Is that the conclusion of your case, Mr Morris?'

'No,' said Wayne smoothly. 'I have one more witness to call. This witness will prove the innocence of my client.'

The DA scowled. The judge scowled. 'I didn't know there was to be any other witness,' said the DA indignantly.

'You know now,' said Wayne. He nodded to his assistant, who got up and crossed to the side door.

'Who is this witness?' asked the judge.

'My assistant's just gone to get her,' said Wayne. 'Her name is Miss Virginia Leighton.'

Virginia Leighton must have been known around Menton. The mention of her name produced surprise in the courtroom. Suddenly, everything became uncertain. The tireless, patient, remorseless waiting of the crowds changed to excited speculation. Everybody was talking at once. The judge, the DA, Wayne and most everybody in court was now looking at the side door.

No stage actress could have wanted a better curtain than Virginia Leighton received when she entered that courtroom.

3

The first thing that struck me about Virginia Leighton, apart from her natural beauty, was the colour of her eyes. Her eyes were green. Not a light green, but the dark, mysterious green of the calm, deep sea.

She entered the courtroom like a queen, her head held high and looking fresh and clean and cool. She was like a breath of cool air in that dry, sweaty atmosphere.

Wayne led her to the witness stand and she stood there taking the oath, her face calm and serene, and somehow she was oblivious of the watching crowd. She was out of place in that courtroom. It seemed almost a crime that a clean-limbed dame like her should be subjected to the oppressive heat of that baking court and the unbearable stench of sweating bodies.

She was wearing a crisp, starched blouse and a flared skirt, and she was a blonde. Her long, fair hair hung almost to her shoulders before it curled in toward her neck. Her hair was parted on the right and looped over her forehead on the other side. Her voice was cool and clear and cut through the thick atmosphere like a bell sounding across the cotton-fields.

The judge was raising his eyebrows at the DA, questioningly. The DA shrugged his shoulders eloquently and hitched his baggy trousers. Wayne invited the girl to sit down and began questioning her. She was certainly a surprise witness.

'Your name is?'

'Virginia Leighton,' she said calmly.

'You live in Menton?'

'I was born here and have lived here all my life,' she said.

'You were acquainted with the deceased?'

'I knew Arthur Kirk well,' she said. There was a lack of emotion in her voice. She answered the questions almost mechanically, and she acted like she and Wayne were the only two in the courtroom. She sat there primly, her knees pressed together and her hands resting in her lap. Her face was upturned to Wayne, awaiting his next question.

'How well did you know the deceased?'

'Lew and Arthur Kirk were my parents' lawyers. When my parents died, Lew and Arthur became my trustees.'

'You mean that your parents' estate is held in trust by them for you?'

She nodded slightly. 'They make me an allowance until I am 25,' she said simply. 'Then the estate passes entirely into my hands.'

'You knew the Kirk brothers well, then?' said Wayne.

'Very well.'

'I'd like you to answer this question,' said Wayne. 'Was there more than a business relationship between yourself and Arthur Kirk?'

For the first time, her answer was not automatic. She hesitated momentarily before she said, 'Not on my side.'

'You mean that Arthur Kirk wanted your relations to be more than friendly?'

'He asked me to marry him,' she said.

'You were engaged to him, then?'

There was a moment's silence. Then she said softly, 'No. We were not engaged.'

'But you were to be engaged?'

Again that moment of hesitation. 'No,' she said. 'I did not accept his proposal.'

That caused a minor sensation in the court. The folks were surprised the dame hadn't wanted to marry Arthur Kirk. The judge banged with his gavel and the mutterings died down.

'Do you know the defendant?' asked Wayne.

The girl looked at Robson, and her face seemed to soften. 'I know Joe Robson,' she said. 'I know him well.'

'And are you aware that he is accused of killing Arthur Kirk on the tenth of this month?'

'Naturally,' she said. A slight smile curved round her lips. The smile seemed to say, *What a silly question.*

'Were you surprised to hear that Joe Robson had been accused of this crime?'

'I was.'

'For any particular reason?'

The judge leaned forward, suddenly tense. The DA's thin, scraggy neck seemed to stretch another six inches as he leaned across his desk. It was so quiet in the courtroom you could hear the grass growing outside.

'I know that Joe Robson did not commit that murder,' she said calmly.

'And how do you know?'

'Because I was with Joe Robson the whole of that night, from nine in the evening until eight the next morning.' I saw her hands clench tightly in her lap and her jaws clamp together. There was a long, strained, unbelieving silence, broken at last by a universal gasp of surprise and disbelief. The judge's mouth gaped wide and the DA's eyes started out of his head. Wayne talked more quickly and more loudly.

'And where were you, Miss Leighton?'

'We were at Joe's shack,' she said calmly. 'I was there with him … all night.' And then she seemed to square her shoulders and lift her head higher to receive bravely the consequences of her admission.

There was immediate pandemonium; the low menacing rumbles of the crowd's disapproval were like the angry sound of an awakening volcano.

The terms of abuse that were hurled at her were unprintable, and one guy behind me shouted over and over again, so loud that I was almost deafened, 'Nigger meat, nigger meat, nigger meat.'

The Deputies sensed the atmosphere and stood shoulder to shoulder across the court. Joe Robson had raised his head and was staring at the girl with eyes that looked like hard-boiled eggs. The judge was pounding with his gavel, and it was strange to see it bouncing off the desk and yet not be able to hear it above the outraged roars of the onlookers.

The girl still sat there, her hands clenched tightly together and her face drawn and set. And then, for the first time, she looked at them. It was a hard, contemptuous look. Those mysterious dark green eyes ranged slowly from one side of the court to the other, slowly, arrogantly, resting, it seemed, in turn upon everybody there. And as though her eyes contained some magic, the angry shouts died away to threatening mumbles.

'Your witness,' said Wayne loudly and distinctly to the DA. He turned sharply on his heel and came back to sit next to me.

'Where d'ya dig her up?' I asked.

'Came to me voluntarily,' he said. 'They can't convict Robson in the face of that testimony.'

The DA must have realised that too. He got up slowly, hitched his baggy trousers around his lean waist and then stood in front of the girl, looking down at the floor and scratching the back of his neck. The crowd was silent now, tense and expectant.

The DA took off his glasses, wiped them on his shirt, and then said quietly, 'This is a kinda shock, Virginia.'

She didn't say anything.

'Why,' he said, sounding surprised, 'I've known you since your father and mother came here when you were just a kid thet high. I guess I didn't ever expect that you was gonna be here telling lies on account of a no-good nigger.'

'I'm not telling lies, Mr Kenley,' she flashed. 'You can't condemn an innocent man to death. I won't let you.'

The judge leaned over his desk with a look of incredulousness on his face. 'Virginia,' he protested, 'You ain't admitting that you're lying to save this durned nigger's skin?'

'I've spoken on oath,' she said. 'Doesn't that mean anything to you?'

'But you couldn't have spent the whole night with this nigger,' he protested.

Her eyes flashed at him scornfully. 'And why not?' she demanded.

That kinda took the wind outta the judge's sails. It kinda took the wind outta the DA's and everybody else's, too.

The DA's address to the jury was a half-hearted, despairing appeal for a conviction. Wayne, on the other hand, made a most moving and telling speech. When the judge summed up, he had no alternative but to give a direction for a not guilty verdict. Now, there was hardly any case at all against Joe Robson, even in his prejudiced eyes.

The court was cleared while the jury retired to make their decision. It was just as well. In another ten minutes, just to draw a breath more of that air would have poisoned me.

Ten minutes later the jury came back and gave their decision of not guilty. But nobody was in the courtroom to hear the decision, because the Sheriff hadn't allowed them to come in again.

When the jury had filed out, the Deputies took Robson back to his cell. Legally he was a free man now. But sending him outside to that waiting crowd would have been like sending him to his death. The judge and the DA conferred in muttered tones, glanced at Virginia Leighton, shook their heads and then went through the side door to the judge's office. That left me and Wayne, his assistant, and Virginia Leighton alone in the courtroom.

'Well,' said Wayne to Virginia, 'we've done it. We've got him off! And we owe everything to you.'

She seemed infinitely weary. The glow was gone from her green eyes. She just said simply, 'What else could I do?'

'It was a mighty fine thing,' said Wayne.

'I think you had real courage,' I said.

Her eyes rested on me for a moment. 'Thank you,' she said, and her voice was almost a whisper.

Wayne's assistant was standing by the windows. 'How does this look to you?' he asked.

We went over and stared out. Some time had elapsed since Virginia Leighton had dropped her bombshell in the courtroom. News travels fast when it travels by word of mouth. The waiting crowd outside must have known by now that Robson had been found innocent. But they were still waiting, still staring at the jail, still expectant and still ominous.

Wayne's forehead puckered. 'I don't like it,' he said.

'They're in a nasty mood.'

'I think I know what they're waiting for,' said Virginia.

'But he's innocent,' I said. 'They surely don't want to lynch an innocent man.'

'It's not Robson they want,' she said quietly. 'It's me.'

I remembered then. Racial discrimination goes deep. The negro who rapes a white woman has asked to be lynched. But there's a balance to the scale. The woman who associates with a negro also earns the resentment of her kind!

4

An hour later the crowd was still there, like a patient beast, waiting to pounce upon its prey.

There were a coupla Deputies with shotguns at the top of the court steps. There wasn't much they could do against the waiting crowd if trouble started. But before they were overpowered they'd be able to inflict some casualties. I guess nobody in the crowd wanted to be the one who'd feel the effects of those shotguns.

The Sheriff came into the courtroom, his boots grinding heavily on the bare boards. Two more Deputies lounged in just behind him. They didn't look very happy. And they looked at Virginia Leighton as though she was a poisonous snake.

The Sheriff's blue eyes flickered, and he spat tobacco juice from the corner of his mouth. He cleared his throat and said coldly, 'I ain't wanting to speak to you, Miss Leighton, except in the line of duty.'

She had hardly spoken all the time we had waited. Her face was controlled and impassive. Her green eyes stared at him calmly. 'You are entitled to choose your company.'

'I aim to do that, ma'am,' he said, with a bite in his voice. His eyes flicked past her as he nodded toward the windows and the waiting crowd outside. 'Ahm speaking in my line of duty, ma'am. Ahm telephoning to Granada for the military. We'll have you and that derned nigger removed under armed escort.'

'Am I under arrest?' she demanded.

'No, ma'am,' he said. 'The law ain't holding you. But I'd be lacking in my duty if I didn't try to give you protection.'

'I don't need your protection,' she said contemptuously.

'Listen, ma'am,' he said. 'You know sure well that you can't leave here ...'

'I don't want your protection,' she repeated.

I interjected quickly, 'How long will it take for the military to get here from Granada?'

He looked at the floor, shuffled his feet and scratched the back of his head. 'You know how it is, mister,' he said. 'Folks around these parts aim to keep the niggers in their place. They could get here in an hour. On the other hand ...' He stroked his chin thoughtfully.

'You mean they might not come?'

He looked at me solemnly. 'Yeah,' he said. 'They might come. Day after tomorrow.'

'I don't need no protection,' repeated Virginia, and holding her head high she walked across the courtroom into the passage toward the entrance.

I went after her, caught her by the arm and spun her around. 'Are you crazy?' I yelled.

Quite calmly she disentangled my hand from her arm. 'Please keep your hands off me,' she said.

'You can't go out there,' I said. 'They'll kill you.'

She looked me over, slowly, calmly. 'You're a stranger here,' she said. 'Perhaps you don't realise. I've lived in this town all my life. Most of the folks out there know me. I've got to live in this town. I've got to see those folks every day. There isn't any point in playing for time. I've got to face them sometime, so I've got to face them now.'

'Miss Leighton,' pleaded Wayne, 'I wish you'd do what the Sheriff suggests.'

'It's my duty,' said the Sheriff sourly. 'I guess I just gotta do my duty.'

Her head went a fraction higher, her green eyes hardened and her face was set. 'Those folks outside are my folks, Sheriff. I've got to face them sometime. I'll face them now.'

We argued with her, we pleaded with her, but her mind was made up. We pleaded with her all the way to the entrance, and then, as she stood at the top of the steps, her head high and her contemptuous eyes ranging slowly over the waiting crowd, I could sense their malignant hatred rolling toward us in great invisible waves.

'We can't let her go,' I said to Wayne.

She heard me. 'If necessary, Sheriff,' she said calmly, 'it will be your duty to arrest anybody interfering with me?'

He looked uncomfortable. 'I guess so, ma'am,' he said.

Once again she shook off my restraining hand. 'Please attend to your own affairs,' she said. 'I'll attend to mine.'

A voice from the crowd called out then. It was strange how quiet the crowd was, and how clearly the one voice could be heard. 'Come on, Virginia. We're waiting for you.'

'You can't do it,' I protested. 'You're crazy.' I took her arm.

The Sheriff's blue eyes glittered. 'Take your hands off her,' he ordered.

I shrugged my shoulders and released her.

She walked down the steps slowly, her head high, her arms hanging by her side and her hands clenched tightly. The Deputies with shotguns moved slightly to allow her to pass. She went down the steps slowly. The crowd watched and waited. The silence of the crowd became a murmur. The murmur became louder and grew to a hungry roar. And suddenly I saw that dame as one of the bravest women I've ever seen. Her chin was still high as she slowly and deliberately walked into the crowd.

At first the crowd was a solid wall of angry, sullen faces, and then, as she got close, miraculously the wall parted, leaving an avenue. I could sense the angry, sullen resistance of that crowd even where I stood. But she had all the grit she needed, and more! Her head was still erect as she walked firmly and steadily into the avenue the crowd made for her. She musta known but chose to ignore the fact that the crowd moved in again, closing the avenue behind her.

Just for a moment I was hoping that nothing would happen.

The mob is always a coward. The mob always waits for a lead, and every individual in the crowd is always waiting for the next man to take that lead. Yeah, I was sap enough to hope that nothing would happen.

And then I saw movement in the crowd. Burly men, farmers, half-a-dozen of them, were shouldering their way through the crowd toward the girl. There was nothing panicky or hurried about their movements, and I guess that was the most unnerving thing about this lynching crowd. There was no panic, no disorder, no sudden eruption into violence. Just a steady patience as though everyone knew that the plans had been made and everything would follow calmly and surely.

The crowd still made a path for the girl. But the burly men shouldering their way through them worked their way in front of her and then stood waiting. When she got to them they were standing shoulder to shoulder. They didn't part. She stood there in front of them, head erect, proud and defiant. She must have said something to them, but it was too far away to hear what it was.

The Sheriff tensed and the two men with shotguns looked up at him. 'Okay, you two,' he said crisply. 'But I don't want no trouble. You know what I mean.'

The two Deputies, shoulder to shoulder, pushed their way into the crowd toward Virginia. It was then I realised just how powerless the Sheriff was. The crowd stood solid. The Deputies pushed and shoved, but they didn't get no place, and the more they shoved, the more they got jolted about themselves.

'Why don't they use their guns?' I asked.

'I'll brain them if they do,' said the Sheriff.

'What the hell …?'

'I'm Sheriff around here,' he interrupted. 'I'm running this town, understand?'

I flicked my eyes to the girl. The six men who seemed to be appointed leaders had moved in on her now. There were three of them on either side of her, and smoothly and easily they took her firmly by the arms. The girl made no attempt to struggle. She stood, head held high and every ounce of her body a contemptuous challenge. She stood there, defiant but unresisting, while they bound her hands firmly together in front of her. The two Deputies had got no nearer toward her, and they'd been jostled so badly that their shirts were torn. Somehow, too, they seemed to have lost their shotguns. They came back out of the crowd, breathing heavily and sweating.

'We can't get no place,' grumbled one of them.

'Forget it,' said the Sheriff. 'Forget it.'

There was more movement now, the crowd parting to make way for a horse and buggy. It forced its way through the crowd massed around the girl and manoeuvred so that she was facing the back of the buggy. There was a six-foot length of slack cord from her pinioned wrists. The tied the end of that to the back of the buggy.

'Where are they taking her?' I demanded anxiously.

The Sheriff spat tobacco juice. 'I wouldn't know,' he said.

'Jeepers,' I yelled. 'They wouldn't lynch a dame, would they?'

'I reckon not,' he said. 'Not a white dame. But I guess maybe they're gonna teach her a lesson.' He spat again. 'Nigger meat, that's what she is. Nigger meat!'

The six men spread out, pressed back the crowds. Virginia's head was still high and her face contemptuous. Even at that distance I thought I could see defiance still glittering in her green eyes.

The buggy jerked forward slowly and the slack of the rope took up suddenly. The girl's pinioned arms came up horizontally, but she still tried to keep her head high and her body erect as she was ignominiously pulled along behind the cart.

The crowd had to make a wide passage to allow for the passing of the buggy. That made it easier for the six men to hold them back. But the crowd didn't seem to need much holding back. It was orderly and patient. It was as though the crowd was content that everything should take its time.

It was a woman who started it. A middle-aged, roughly-dressed woman with unkempt hair and lean, sun-browned arms. She broke through the crowd, sprang savagely at Virginia and bore her to the ground. I saw her ripping and tearing, and as they pulled her away, she took with her part of Virginia's blouse. Virginia was down, sprawled on the ground, while the relentless motion of the buggy dragged her through the dust, scraping the skin from her body and legs. The milky white skin of her shoulders and back showed where the blouse had been torn.

The first spark had flown. A howl went up. The crowd changed in an instant from passive remorselessness to action-hungry beasts. Those at the back were yelling for those who were nearest to 'strip the bitch'.

The crowd closed in on Virginia. She went down beneath the weight of them. The buggy was dragged to a standstill and the crowd was roaring and shouting, waving their fists and stamping. The six men who had pinioned Virginia's arms were in there, too, fighting savagely, fighting to get Virginia away from angry, rending fingers.

I went ice-cold. This was something I just couldn't stand by and see. I said to the Sheriff, 'Give me your revolver.'

His blue eyes looked at me. For a second I thought he wasn't going to do anything. Then his hand went to his side, and he drew his revolver.

But he didn't give it to me. Instead he pointed it at my belly. 'I don't want no trouble, mister,' he said.

I breathed hard. 'You can stand by and see murder, if you like,' I said. 'I ain't no Sheriff. But I'm a decent citizen. I've got to do what I can to stop this.'

His Deputies had drawn their revolvers too. They trained them on me and Wayne. The Sheriff said slowly, 'That crowd's dynamite. It needs just one little spark and they'll be shedding blood. Plenty of blood. Half of them are armed. There's a gas station over the way. If you try crossing that crowd there'll be real trouble.'

'Okay,' I said bitterly. 'If that's the way you want it, I'll do it with my bare hands. At any rate, I will have tried.'

He pressed his revolver forward until the barrel dug into my side. 'I'm warning you,' he said grimly. 'You walk down those steps and by God I'll put a bullet in your leg. You can take it or leave it, fella. But I ain't letting you start a riot that we'll never be able to stop.'

I looked into his blue, slitted eyes. But there was nothing I could do about it. He meant every word he said.

My lips had gone suddenly dry. I licked them with a tongue that was like sandpaper. Getting a bullet in my leg wasn't going to help that dame. On the other hand, standing there, watching, wasn't going to help much either.

A sudden loud roar from the crowd drew my attention back to what was going on.

The six men had managed to get Virginia clear of the clutches of the crowd. But the crowd was willing to leave her alone now. As they pressed back, leaving a circle around her, she was helped to her feet. She was as naked as the day she was born, and loud brutal shouts of scorn and derision mocked her as torn fragments of her clothing were tossed above the heads of the mob.

A coupla men helped her to her feet, but the horrors of the last few moments had stripped the girl of all her defiance. She crouched now, her head bowed, her pinioned hands held high to cover her breasts and her white body flinching beneath the hungry, merciless eyes that gloatingly probed her young body and ruthlessly robbed her of her most intimate modesties.

And the great crowd became silent now, as though partly ashamed of her humiliation. And yet the anger was still there, simmering and waiting for yet something more to happen.

The driver roared to his horse, the buggy jerked forward and the girl was tugged along behind. She was wearing only one shoe, and at the third step she stumbled. She fell on her side and the buggy moved on relentlessly, dragging her over the rough ground. Desperately she struggled to her feet, tearing the skin from her knees, while the crowd watched mercilessly. Nobody offered to help her. When she did get to her feet she had lost her other shoe.

Her head hung, her long fair hair was like a cloud shielding her shamed face from the stares of the crowd. But her white body was an open book, shamelessly exposed as the buggy rolled on and the great crowd followed behind. They were heading toward the far end of the town, toward the open country.

The Sheriff kept his gun boring into my ribs until the square in front of the courthouse was cleared and all we could see was the back of the crowd moving in a steady, relentless mass out of sight.

'Sheriff,' I said heavily. 'If anything happens to that girl, it'll mean your neck.'

His blue eyes were hard and clear. 'I know my duty,' he said. 'You can't stop folks around here doing what they want when they're set on it. And right now, I've more than one problem on my mind.' He looked at the two Deputies who had lost their shotguns. 'You've got your chance now, fellas,' he said. 'While there's nobody around, get a car and get that doggorn nigger outta here. Drop him over the State line somewhere.'

'Just how long are you gonna keep pressing that revolver in my belly?' I asked.

'Just so long as I see fit,' he snarled. 'And I mean what I say. I'm ready to shoot anytime, to save a riot.'

I looked at Wayne. 'What does the law say about this?'

He shrugged. 'I guess it's a kinda emergency. He's entitled to use his discretion. I guess it's true what he says. A spark is liable to start a riot. Then he might have a mess.'

I waited and fumed until the two Deputies got back with the car. They got Robson from the cells and bundled him inside and set off outta town in the opposite direction to the crowd. As soon as they'd got clear, the Sheriff stuck his revolver back in his holster.

'Now there ain't no cause for them to come burning down the court,' he said with satisfaction. 'There ain't no durned nigger here for them to get a hold of.'

I started down the steps.

'Where you going?' asked the Sheriff.

'I'm going to do what I can for that girl.'

'Wait for me,' he said. 'I'll be along.'

The Sheriff and the two Deputies disappeared into the building. I looked at Wayne angrily. 'You could have saved the girl all this,' I said. 'You didn't have to put her on the stand.'

'But truth is truth,' he protested. 'They'd have given a verdict of guilty against Robson if I hadn't.'

I smiled bitterly. 'What's the good of justice in a place like this? They'd have lynched Robson anyway, guilty or not guilty, if the dame hadn't been so damned crazy as to walk out there.'

He nodded wryly. 'I guess justice is one thing,' he admitted, 'and human behaviour is another.'

'That dame's in a spot, Wayne,' I said. 'We've gotta get her out of it some way. We aren't going to get much help from the Sheriff. It's just up to you and me.'

'How?' asked Wayne 'It looks pretty hopeless. There's just two of us against them. And we ain't even got a gun.'

I thought quickly. I got out my car keys and thrust them in his hand. 'We've got just one chance,' I said. 'Surprise action. The only way we can break through that crowd to release her is with a car.'

'Meaning what?'

'Get back to the carpark. Get my car as soon as you can. Follow the crowd. Drive through the crowd. Run them down if necessary. Run as close to the girl as you can.'

'What will you be doing?'

'I'll be up there somewhere. If anything happens before you arrive, I'll play for time. But I'm relying on you. Our only hope is to get the girl in the car and break our way out.'

'Look after yourself,' he said.

'There's just one more thing,' I said. 'There's a toolbox let into the floorboards under the carpet in the back seat. I always keep my Luger there.' I looked at him meaningfully. 'It'd be handy to have that around.'

'I get you,' he said. He set off up the street, walking quickly. He had about ten minutes' walk in front of him. It'd take him maybe five minutes to find my car. And there was no saying how long it would take him to get out of the carpark. He'd maybe have to shift a dozen other cars out of his way.

One of the Deputies strolled out of the building onto the front steps just then. He screwed up his eyes against the glare of the sun and squinted after Wayne. 'Where's he going?'

'Just remembered he wants to visit the car,' I said. At the same time, my eyes slipped down to the revolver he wore at his side. Suddenly my fingers began to itch to close around the butt of that gun.

'The Sheriff gonna be long?' I asked casually.

'About five minutes.'

'Where are they taking her to?' I asked, nodding after the crowd.

Automatically he stared in that direction. His arms were at his side and his jaw was outlined perfectly. He didn't even gasp. The only sound was the sharp clop as my knuckles smashed against his jaw, followed by the soft sound of his body slumping on the steps.

I'd stepped a long way out of line this time. Socking a cop could get me fourteen days in the pen. But I wasn't thinking about going to jail. I was thinking about that poor dame.

I loosened the revolver from his holster, checked it to make sure it was loaded, and dropped it into my pocket.

The Deputy looked untidy. I straightened him up, propped him against the wall like he was sleeping in the sun, and then started running. I ran in the direction the crowd had taken. I was scared what they was gonna do to that dame, and I was scared what might happen to me.

I was one man against a blood-hungry mob. I was one man alone and with just six bullets in my gun. And I was scared right down to the pit of my belly.

But I kept running. I kept running into trouble, toward trouble. And although I was as scared as hell, I just couldn't help myself.

5

They hadn't gone far, just around the bend out of town and into a pasture field. I had the feeling everything had been organised. There'd been time for it. A couple of hours had elapsed between the time when Virginia had entered the court and when she had proudly and bravely walked out into the waiting crowd.

It was a big field. The crowd was massed over to the left of it. The ground there sloped down into a great basin. It formed a natural amphitheatre. The buggy drawing the girl had been driven down to the bottom of the basin and the crowd gathered around. Everybody could get a perfect view of what was about to happen.

My heart was thumping madly and I was sweating so much that my clothes were sticking to me. I shouldered my way into that crowd. Shouldered my way roughly and aggressively. I was in no mood for being trifled with, and I guess my face showed it. Lots of fellas grunted and glared, but nobody tried to get tough. I elbowed and shouldered my way right through the crowd until I was in the forefront. Then I just stood there like the rest of the crowd, watching. My heart was pounding and my mouth was as dry as a bag of sawdust.

Everyone was standing well back, leaving a wide circle. In the centre of the circle was the buggy. The girl was still tied to it and she was kneeling on the ground, huddled up to preserve her modesty. I couldn't see her face, because her head was bowed and her long hair rippled across her cheeks and shoulders. There was an ugly scratch stretching from her shoulder-blade down to the small of her back.

This thing had been organised. About twenty fellas were spaced around the circle, their arms extended and pushing back the crowd when it threatened to advance too far. But the crowd was orderly. Waiting and expectant. Its appetite had been kindled. It was waiting for the feast.

I saw right away what was going to happen. There were six fellas wearing leather aprons and rubber overalls. A couple of them wore long gloves reaching to the elbow. Much more significant was the great, chest-high barrel of thick tar.

I cocked my ear and listened for the sound of an approaching car. Just how far this was gonna go, I daren't think. But, alone, I had as much chance as a celluloid cat in hell. I was up against a wild, angry mob. A show of firearms wasn't going to get me anything except, maybe, a bullet between my shoulders. And once the shooting started, anything might happen; especially to the dame.

The crowd began to roar now; they wanted action. They were tired of waiting.

A coupla guys wearing overalls went over to Virginia. They untied her wrists, pulled her to her feet and, holding her by the arms, dragged her toward the great barrel of tar.

I don't think until that moment she had realised what was going to happen. As soon as she saw that barrel and realised its significance, her green eyes filled with horror. She began to struggle desperately. The other four men lent a hand. They held her by her arms, her body and legs. She struggled and screamed but, remorselessly, they carried her toward the barrel.

It was then that the voice of the crowd made itself heard in earnest. There was a kinda wild frenzy about that howling, blood-lusting crowd. They roared with fiendish excitement. It was mass hysteria. The voice of the crowd sounded in my ears like the baying of hounds must sound to the exhausted, hunted stag. They carried her, lifted her chest-high, and held her poised, feet down over the barrel. And then the crowd grew silent, as though determined to enjoy every moment and every sound, unwilling even to miss the high-pitched shriek of the victim.

I concentrated all my faculties on listening for the sound of the car. The crowd was grimly silent, so silent that I could hear the birds singing in the distant treetops. But I didn't hear a car.

And right then I knew there was nothing I could do for her. I could only wait and hope.

They lowered her, feet first, and her body recoiled and arched as her dainty white feet met the tar. She was screaming madly now. They lowered her slowly and remorselessly. Her feet disappeared up to the ankles and the black tide spread slowly up her calves.

The tar musta been almost cold. It was thick, sluggish, like mud. The crowd gave a huge sigh, like a sigh of pain ... or ecstasy. And the tar was so thick that the men were bearing their weight to press her down into it.

I felt weak, as though all the strength had been drained outta me, and together with the sensation of my utter powerlessness, there came over me a kinda ugly fascination. I glanced around at the faces on either side. I saw no pity, no anger, but, instead, a kinda evil concentration. Hard-set faces were expressionless, but malicious eyes glared hungrily, absorbing every single movement.

Virginia was still screaming, straining and arching he back in a desperate attempt to get free. Strong hands were holding her body firmly, almost brutally, and the thick tar, now above her knees, was clogging the frantic movements of her legs.

I wanted to look away, shut my ears to the sound of her screams, or wade right in there and try to stop this thing from happening. But the voice of reason was urging me to keep cool, await my moment and act quickly and smoothly. Snatching the girl outta this crowd was gonna be a whole lot more dangerous than snatching a bone from a hunger-crazed dog.

The tar was mounting up her thighs now, higher and higher. Her struggles became even more desperate. I listened again, and still there was no car. The tar was high up her thighs now. I closed my eyes. A few moments later her screams seemed to redouble in their intensity. When I reopened my eyes the black tide was lapping over the white skin of her belly. She'd stopped screaming now, as though exhausted. Her green eyes stared down, horror-stricken, as blackness enveloped her white flesh. She still struggled, although she knew it was hopeless.

They lowered her until the tar had risen, half-covering her young, white breasts, until the displacement caused by her body made the tar run over. She stood there, immersed to the armpits, clinging desperately to the side of the barrel.

The tallest of the men leaned over the barrel. He rested his gloved hands on her white shoulders and pressed down hard. She tried to resist him, tried to squirm away, but he was strong and she was already exhausted. Her knees musta given beneath his weight, and as the tar came up to her chin, she scrabbled desperately with her fingers.

But the man was merciless. He was unmoved by her mute, appealing eyes, by her long, glistening fair hair already besmirched. He transferred one hand to the crown of her head and levered hard. It happened quickly then. Her head went out of sight and his arm disappeared up to the elbow.

He stepped back, and a moment later her tar-covered head broke the surface. She'd become a wild, unrecognisable black monster. Black, shapeless arms clawed at her mouth and nostrils. She was whimpering, making strange gutteral noises; the tar, like thick mud, oozed in a leaden stream from the top of the barrel as she scrabbled like some wild beast.

I was sweating so bad that it was running into my eyes, blinding me. I wiped the sweat away, and my hands were shaking. My nerves were shrieking. I wasn't going to be able to stand this much longer. And still there was no sound of an approaching car!

They were dragging big sacks to the foot of the barrel. They opened the sacks, upended them. Dirty flock, cheap upholstery stuffing, flowed from the mouth of the sack. It formed a carpet a foot deep. The grotesque black figure was still uttering those strange animal noises and clawing at the rim of the barrel, trying to draw itself free from the thick, sucking tar. The big fella, the one who had shoved her head beneath the surface, leaned his weight against the barrel. His face reddened and his biceps swelled as he pushed. Slowly the barrel toppled and then crashed onto its side. Like a thick river of lead, the tar oozed sluggishly from the barrel. They pulled the barrel to one side, leaving Virginia clawing herself to her feet. One of them shoved her so that she sprawled into the mixture of tar and flock. And then they were heaping the flock on her. They covered her with it, rolled her over and over, plastered her from head to toe, until there wasn't a square inch of her tar-coated body that was visible beneath the flock coating.

What agonies of humiliation the girl was suffering, I wouldn't even try to imagine. But she musta been pretty near to exhaustion by the time they'd finished. When they were finally through, they had to pull her to her feet by the arms and hold her while the waiting crowd surveyed her with satisfaction.

She was a grotesque sight. A shapeless tar-and-flock-encrusted shape that could have been man or woman or beast. The crowd went crazy, shouting, jeering and yelling. It hadn't been such a bad day for them after all. They'd expected a lynching. But tarring and feathering a dame was almost as good fun!

The men holding Virginia let go her arms so that she could slump on the ground. She lay there, grovelling in tar that was too thick to soak into the dry earth. A coupla guys who'd been handling her stood watching, while the others prepared to leave.

What was the next step, I wondered? What else, if anything, could be added to the torment already endured by Virginia? The obvious thing was to leave her now. Leave her the way she was, humiliated and sullied. Leave her to blindly grope her way home. As she fumbled her way along the Main Street she'd suffer all over again the humiliation she'd just experienced. Maybe some kind person, unable to stand the sight of her suffering, would try to help her and for his pains become another victim of the crowd.

But the sadistic hunger of the crowd had been aroused. The

voice of the crowd was howling, shouting and clamouring for yet another spectacle.

Hard knuckles dug into my kidneys. I turned my head and found myself staring into the hard blue eyes of the Sheriff. His brows were beetled and his face set and hard.

'I'm wanting a word with you,' he said, his voice hard and biting. I knew what was on his mind. I'd slugged one of his Deputies and taken his gun.

'You're a duty-loving Sheriff,' I sneered. 'You seem to be lagging behind in your work.' I jerked my head in the direction of the tortured, grotesque figure of Virginia. 'How come you let that kinda thing happen?'

The hard blue eyes narrowed. 'I run this town the way I see fit,' he gritted. 'Right now I'm charging you with ...'

His voice was drowned out by the renewed roaring of the crowd. The shout had first started somewhere over the far side. Just one fella musta shouted in the first place. Then those nearby had taken up the shout. Then it had spread, rapidly being taken up by the rest of the spectacle-ravenous mob. And as the shout of the mob became a steady, rhythmical chant, I distinguished the words, and a big, cold toad began to stir in the pit of my belly. I glanced at the Sheriff, and his hard blue eyes had slitted even more.

The crowd was chanting over and over again, '*Fire. Fire. We want fire!*'

Yeah, there was more that could be done to that dame. Just to leave her to grope herself home wasn't enough for that mob. They wanted to see her burning alive, a human torch, running madly in circles as the tar and flock burned her pain-wracked body. They wanted to see her, a human torch, running, dancing, rolling in agony. 'Jeepers,' I said aloud, and found that the sweat running down my face was ice-cold.

The fellas with the leather aprons consulted together. They shot occasional glances at the dame still grovelling on the ground. The voice of the crowd still chanted. '*Fire. Fire. We want fire!*' I saw a coupla men shake their heads vigorously. The crowd redoubled its strength and yelled even louder. '*Fire. Fire.*

We want fire!'

A couple of the guys shrugged their shoulders. They talked some more and then seemed to reach a decision. Slowly and deliberately they walked outta the circle and joined the crowd, where they stood waiting and watching.

Their gesture was clear enough. They weren't willing to turn the dame into a torch. But if that was what the crowd wanted, they were willing and ready to watch.

'You've gotta stop this,' I said to the Sheriff, desperately.

'Are you crazy?'

'You've gotta try, anyway,' I said.

He grunted. That was all.

The crowd was still chanting. The dame had climbed to her feet. She stood there, unseeing and weak, swaying and ready to drop at any moment, and her life hung by a thread. The crowd was there, waiting and willing, tensed and ready for anything. It needed just one man or group of men to start and the crowd would be with them. Just across the other side of the circle, three men stepped forward. There were ugly grins on their faces as one of them held a rolled newspaper to the flame of a cigarette lighter. The newspaper flared high, and the voice of the crowd was a maddened, excited and insane roar.

This was it. In another few seconds the dame would be a human torch, with the flames leaping over her body from head to toe. In four quick strides I was into the circle. The guy holding the flaming newspaper was so excited he never knew what hit him. His nose squelched like a tomato as I planted my fist in his face, with every ounce of my hate and detestation lending extra power to the blow. He hurtled back into the crowd and brought a coupla other guys down with him.

I wasn't going to get far fighting that crowd with my bare fists. I levelled my gun and swept it in a wide arc. The sun glinted and flashed on the long barrel. The sight of it stopped the forward surge of the crowd. A thick, awful silence descended. I stood there in that circle, the gun in my hand and thousands of angry, outraged eyes fixed upon me. One man against thousands. One small gun against hundreds. And I was as scared as hell. There was ice trickling down my spine, my knees were trembling and my mouth was so dry I thought I wasn't gonna be able to speak. But I managed to rasp, loudly enough for those near me to hear, 'The first who makes a move is gonna get it.'

That's a fine thing to say when you're completely surrounded and any number of guys can pump lead in between your shoulder-blades. I circled quickly, letting everybody see that gun. I had to keep my head and my eyes moving all the time. Just what was gonna happen next, I didn't know. Just for a few seconds, maybe, I'd keep this crowd awed by the suddenness of my action, and by the sight of the gun.

I'd done a crazy thing. Without the car there wasn't a hope in hell of getting outta there. Even if I didn't earn a bullet, there was still plenty of tar and flock. The crowd was in the mood to appreciate two human dancing torches.

Somebody started. From way behind me a revolver cracked. A bullet tore into the ground a coupla yards to my left. I spun around and fired over the heads of the crowd. There was a kinda stampede as folks tried to get outta the way.

That was when the Sheriff came into the picture. Slowly, unhurried, and with his guns in his hands, he paced into the tiny circle. Just the sight of him seemed to restore some order. The panic stopped. His hard blue eyes roved around watchfully, but he spoke quietly, so that only I could hear. 'Stand with your back to me,' he said. 'We can cover both sides that way.'

It was comforting to feel his hard shoulders against mine. It took away that uneasy feeling that I was about to have lead plugging into my back. The crowd was shocked, silent. The Sheriff raised his voice and said loudly:

'There ain't no more, folks. Go on home now and don't cause no more trouble.'

Voices yelled at him: 'Get outta the way, Sheriff.'

'This ain't your business. Don't you start something.'

'We can burn you and all.'

Somewhere, somebody started the chant again. The crowd

took it up more slowly this time. But the ugly menace was there just the same. '*Fire. Fire. We want fire.*'

The Sheriff growled over his shoulder. 'You durned fool. Now you've started something. There'll be a riot. You can't cross up a crowd like this.'

'Get the hell outta it,' I gritted. 'I'll handle this alone.'

When he replied, his voice had softened. 'Jeepers, you're a crazy guy. But I like your guts. I'll stay in this deal.'

A loud voice like the bellow of a bull rang out. It cut across the chant of the crowd. 'We're giving you and that other fella three minutes to get outta here, Sheriff. After that, we're gunning for you.'

'See what I mean?' he said over his shoulder. 'Are you gonna be smart?'

I licked my dry lips. 'I can't do it,' I said. 'Whatever happens, I can't let them do it. It's murder.'

'Heaven help us,' he said quietly. 'They're blood-mad. They mean what they say, and ...'

The voice of the mob had stopped me hearing it before. But I heard it now. The sound of a car. The sound of a car driven furiously and recklessly. The noise of it travelled on the clear, hot air like the sound of a motorboat carrying across the water.

The heads of the crowd turned in the direction of the sound. And then the crowd was scattering madly, jumping, falling, stumbling, scrabbling to get out of the way of the heavy car that raced at them like a jet-plane going into a power-dive.

Miraculously the crowd cleared a path for the inrushing car. The car swerved violently and squealed to a halt in a cloud of dust.

The Sheriff didn't know anything about this. But I did. Even before the car had stopped, I'd grabbed Virginia and had bundled her into the vehicle.

The Sheriff was gaping.

'Get in, man,' I yelled. 'Get in.'

So sudden and unexpected had been the arrival of the car that the crowd was stunned. But those amongst it who were quick-witted and grasped what was happening surged forward.

Their roar was the angry snarl of a predator cheated of its prey.

I almost shoved the Sheriff into the front seat of the car beside Wayne Morris, and the car was moving again even before I'd climbed into the back seat alongside Virginia.

The crowd surged forward, angry hands grasped at the car, trying to hold it back. It wasn't so easy to build up speed now. The car was at the foot of the natural depression. I saw Wayne clench his teeth as he stamped his foot on the accelerator and fingered the horn. The crowd got out of our way. That was natural. Nobody deliberately stands in front of a car to be run down. But they hung onto the sides like grapes clustered on a vine. The sheer dead weight of those clinging bodies was almost fatal. The engine groaned and spluttered as it tried to nose its way up the slope. And they were trying to get the doors open, tugging at the handles, trying to pull down the glass windows. Somebody was hanging on the running-board with a rock in his hand. He was pounding the rock against the window. The window was specially treated to prevent flying fragments. It cracked and splintered like a spider's web. And the fella kept pounding with the rock. He kept pounding at the weak spot. Sooner or later that window would give.

The engine was quivering and straining. The car shook and quivered beneath the weight of bodies, and as we were about to crest the slope, for one awful moment it seemed the engine would stall, unable to take the strain.

But it did take the strain. For a few anxious seconds the car was almost at a standstill. And then it crested the slope, and on the level ground began to gather speed.

It gathered speed slowly. It wasn't surprising. There musta been a coupla dozen of them hanging on, trailing behind, trying to slow it up. I looked through the back window, and the crowd was flooding around us. Angry faces, upraised hands and drawn guns. I guess the only reason no shooting took place was for fear of hitting the fellas hanging onto the car. For some seconds it looked like we'd be unable to outstrip the crowd. But the engine responded magnificently. Slowly we picked up speed. Slowly, painfully, we drew ahead of the running crowd, and then, as our speed mounted, Wayne began to swerve violently. Every time he swerved, a couple fellas were thrown clear. It was like a dog shaking itself to get rid of fleas. And as we shook them off, the speed of the car correspondingly increased.

There was one fella who'd climbed onto the roof of the car. He was lying there, holding on tenaciously. He was still there after all the others had been shaken loose. Wayne got rid of him by deliberately driving at full speed over a mole-hill. The car bumped so high that our heads touched the roof. When I looked through the back window, the guy who'd been on the top of the car still hadn't hit the ground. And when he did hit the ground, he just lay there.

The crowds were a long way behind now. They weren't chasing no more. They were just standing, shaking their fists. Wayne drove on, straight across the field to the other side, where, fortunately, there was a gate onto a secondary road.

The Sheriff said: 'That's far enough for me. You can drop me.'

'What are you going to do?' I asked.

His hard blue eyes looked at me directly. 'I'm gonna forget you hit my Deputy,' he said. 'That's a charge that can lie over.'

'I don't mean that,' I said. I jerked my head in the direction from which we had just come. 'What are you going to do about that?'

He grinned. 'Party's over, I guess. You've got the star performer.' He glanced at Virginia. 'Although what in hell you're gonna do with her, I don't know. You sure had better keep her well clear of Menton. The next time, she won't be so lucky.'

I looked at Virginia and shuddered. 'What the hell am I gonna do with her?'

'That's your problem,' he said. 'You started this, reckon you'll have to finish it.'

Wayne got out from behind the steering wheel. 'Reckon I'll be leaving you here, too, Hank,' he said.

'Where are you goin'?'

'I'm going back with the Sheriff.' His jaw hardened and his eyes glittered. 'There's legal matters to be dealt with. Questions of a malicious prosecution that was not proven. Maybe Robson won't be able to live in Menton again. But I'm gonna make sure he gets enough compensation to live comfortably somewhere else.'

'You're gonna be mighty unpopular in town,' said the Sheriff.

Wayne grinned at him. 'Just about as popular as you, I guess. Maybe we ought to stick together until things quieten down.'

The Sheriff's hard blue eyes surveyed Wayne for a moment. And then the hardness turned to softness. The corners of his mouth crinkled, and for the first time, I saw him grin. 'Okay, fella,' he grinned. 'We'll stick together.' He turned to me. 'My advice to you, fella,' he said. 'Just get in that driving-seat and keep driving. Get as far as you can from here, as quickly as you can.'

That was good sound advice I hadn't needed. I was still sweating. I didn't wanna go through that again. I didn't really begin to feel easy until I'd put twenty miles between myself and Menton.

And, being a selfish kinda guy, I began to feel thankful I'd got outta that without too much trouble. Even began to feel a little pleased with myself for being such a smart, brave fella, even though I'd been a little scared at the time.

Yeah, that's the kinda selfish guy I was. Thinking about myself all the time. It wasn't until the dame on the back seat gave a long shuddering moan that I began to think about her for a change.

And that required thinking about. Just to have a dame on your hands with no place to go was bad enough. But a dame in that condition! Tarred and feathered beyond recognition, spattering the inside of my car with tar I'd never get off and probably sticking to the upholstery. What did I do with her?

There I was again. Thinking about myself. It wasn't pleasant, but I forced myself to think just how that poor dame must be feeling herself.

She musta felt like hell. And what could be done about it?

Yeah, there was the rub. Just what could be done about it?

6

I guess that dreadful experience had exhausted Virginia. She lay there in the back, semi-conscious, not moving and her breath rasping. There was nothing she could do for herself, and nothing I could do right then to help.

I was driving through open country with a river over on my left and thick woodland between us and the river. I stopped the car, got a blanket from the trunk and covered it over the girl. Then I drove on again and stopped at the next garage. It was only a small filling-station with just one pump. The attendant came out and automatically removed the gas-tank cap to insert the nozzle. I let him pump gasoline into the tank until it was full and then said: 'I want some gasoline in cans.'

His eyebrows raised. 'In cans?'

'Yeah,' I said. 'I'll pay for the cans.'

I propped open the lid of the trunk and calculated. 'About half-a-dozen jerry cans, I guess.'

He whistled. 'Twenty-five gallons! You must be going a long way.'

'I hate stopping,' I said shortly.

He musta thought I was crazy. He kept giving me sidelong glances as he filled the jerry-cans and stowed them in the trunk. When he was through I asked: 'Do you keep cotton-waste around for cleaning?'

'Sure, we got a little. How much do you want?'

'How much you got?'

He kinda gaped at me. He was sure I was nuts now. He mentally shrugged his shoulders and said, 'Come see for yourself.'

I followed him to the repair shack, and at the back he had a large sack stuffed with cotton-waste. 'Give me a large armful,' I said.

That was too much for him. 'Look, mister,' he said, 'just so I don't get the jitters, will you let me see your dough first?'

I took out my wallet, peeled off enough bills to cover the gasoline, the cotton-waste and twenty for him and thrust them into his hand. 'Now, how about a little action?' I said.

The dough answered all questions. He tucked it away eagerly, grabbed himself a big armful of cotton-waste and carried it to the car.

He wedged it in and around the jerry-cans. While he was doing it, I shot a quick look inside the car. Virginia was lying there, still covered by the blanket.

I closed the trunk as the attendant stood watching me.

He said: 'You got tar on your clothes.'

I grinned. 'A lotta guys decided they'd like to tar and feather me.'

He grinned back. He thought it was a joke. 'You'll have a job getting that off.'

'I'll manage.'

I drove slowly for a few miles, looking for a likely spot. I found it eventually. I ran the car off the road and in among the trees. It was tricky going, but by using the steering- wheel furiously and going into reverse frequently I managed to work the car twenty to thirty yards into the woods and within a few yards of the river.

We were well off the road and out of sight. The foliage was thick and green and the birds sang happily, undisturbed by the occasional roar of a passing car. The river glided past smoothly, catching the rays of the sun and throwing it back in a thousand broken fragments. A light, warm breeze sent ripples racing across the water and lapping and chuckling along the river bank.

I got the girl out of the back of the car. She was huddled up, face in hands, shoulders bowed despondently, and somehow I sensed the utter despair she was suffering. I won't try to describe what she looked like. She looked hardly even human, in an obscene kinda way.

I steered her across to the riverbank and sat her down. She kinda hunched there with her knees under her chin and her face buried in her hands. I went back to the car and got a can of gasoline and a thick wad of cotton-waste.

When I got back to her, I said, 'It's gonna take time, sister. But you're gonna be all right.'

She acted like she hadn't heard.

'Hey,' I said loudly. 'D'you hear me?'

She still made no answer.

I pulled the blobs that were her hands away from her head and yelled even louder. 'Hey. Can you hear me?'

I was a dope. Of course she couldn't hear me. Her ears were plugged with tar. She couldn't hear a thing. She couldn't see, either. Even her nostrils were clogged with tar. And the tar was drying so rapidly maybe she wouldn't be able to move herself about if it hardened too much.

I rolled her over on her side so I could get at her ear.

She resisted me. She didn't know where she was. For all she knew, she was back there in the field, about to undergo yet some other torment.

I clawed as much of the tar away from her as I could and then soaked the cotton-waste in gasoline. It was ticklish work. It's said you should never put anything in your ear smaller than your elbow. Her ear was full of thick, hardening tar. It was a nasty job and a messy job. I guess she must have realised how I was trying to help, because she lay there passively. When I got the ear clean I said: 'Can you hear me now?'

She nodded mutely. 'I'm blind,' she said. 'They've blinded me.'

'Let's have a look,' I said gently.

She wasn't blind. But the tar was so thick and tenacious that her eyelids were glued together. 'Keep still,' I warned her. 'Keep your eyes clenched tight until I tell you to open them. This ain't going to be pleasant.'

I worked on her eyes, got them clean. Swabbed the eyelids with gasoline and softened her long eyelashes, washing away the tar. Then I dabbed her eyes with the cotton-waste.

'Okay,' I said. 'You can open now.'

Her eyes opened slowly, blinking against the smart of the gasoline. It gave me a kinda minor thrill to see just how green her eyes were. But it almost broke my heart to see the dull, pained, despairing expression in those beautiful eyes.

'You're all right now,' I said softly. 'We're right away from there now.'

'I want to die,' she said quietly. 'Why didn't they kill me?'

'You're all right now,' I said gently. 'You'll forget all about this in no time.'

She propped herself up on one elbow and looked down at her body. She gave a gasp of horror. 'What have they done to me?' she moaned.

'Nothing that can't be put right with some elbow grease,' I said cheerfully. 'Give me your arm.'

Automatically she held up her arm. I scraped her arm with a broad stick, and the tar and the flock peeled off. But only the top layer. Beneath, the tar had dyed her flesh like a second skin. I had to rub vigorously with a gasoline-soaked pad before the pink of her flesh began to show through.

'See what I mean?' I said. 'We'll fix this in no time.'

She gave a kinda sob.

'You've had a tough time, sister,' I said. 'Just you lay back and leave it to me.'

She lay back as though exhausted. I went over her with a broad stick, scraping off the worst of it. It was a long job. My hands and forearms were plastered with tar up to the elbows by the time I had worked down to her feet.

'Don't worry, sister,' I encouraged. 'It won't be long now.'

I almost rubbed her raw, cleaning up her face, neck and shoulders. There wasn't a thing I could do about her hair. It was matted together and stuck hard like a tarred rope. I had to hack it off short with a penknife and soak what was left in gasoline, leaving it to dry off. Doing that much used four gallons of gasoline. I took the empty can back to the car and got out another. I didn't leave her for more than a coupla minutes, but when I turned around she was wading into the river. Thigh deep, hip deep, chest deep.

I went running back. 'Hey,' I yelled. 'You can't wash that stuff off.'

She took no notice of me. She breasted the water and floundered out where it was deep.

'Hey,' I yelled again. 'Tar won't wash off.'

Her head bobbed up above the water and then disappeared. It was a long while before it reappeared – an inordinately long time. And when it disappeared again, I realised what was happening.

I swore softly to myself as I kicked off my shoes. I was still swearing as I ran down the bank and plunged in. I got to her just as she bobbed up for the third time. She was making no effort to save herself, not even struggling.

I grabbed her by the shoulders and towed her back to the bank. I sprawled in the shallow water, breathing hard. She was coughing and spluttering beside me. She'd got a lotta that river in her lungs.

'You're crazy,' I said.

'Why didn't you leave me?' she pleaded. 'I wanna die. I've got nothing to live for.'

'You're crazy,' I repeated irritably. 'Just because you get a little dirt smeared over you.'

She coughed and spluttered some more. I got up and pulled her to her feet.

'Don't let's have any more of this nonsense,' I said.

'Why are you interfering? Why don't you leave me,' she demanded piteously. 'I want to die. Why won't you let me die?'

I thrust a wad of gasoline-soaked cotton-waste in her hand. 'Don't waste time feeling sorry for yourself,' I gritted. 'Let's see some action.'

'I wanna die,' she moaned.

'Okay,' I said. 'You wanna die. That's okay by me. But you can do that later. Right now, you're gonna get yourself cleaned up.'

'For god's sake leave me alone,' she moaned, and lay back.

One way and another this dame was causing me plenty of grief. Not only had I got my clothes tarred all over, but now they were soaking wet, too.

I breathed hard. 'All right,' I said bitterly. 'Leave me to do it all. I'm a sucker.'

I've sandpapered wood to get it smooth and French-polished it to get a veneer effect. I've scrubbed a boat-deck until it was as clean as a new pin, gleaming whitely in the hot sun. But the amount of labour I had to put into those jobs was as nothing compared with the amount of elbow-grease I had to put in on that dame. I washed her in gasoline, soaked her in gasoline, practically floated her in gasoline. I laboured and sweated until my clothes steamed and dried on my body and my arm muscles became sore and tired. I soaked, sponged, rubbed and combed her hair until she screamed with the pain of it, and until the silky texture was apparent once again.

But my labour was worthwhile. It showed results. And as her soft skin, glowing now from my urgent rubbing, began to come clean, she lost her despondency. She, too, began to scrub at herself, soaking the cotton-waste swabs with gasoline and rubbing furiously, until it seemed the skin itself would come away.

The question of maidenly modesty entered neither of our heads. Natural modesty had been stripped away from her, together with her clothes, back there in Menton.

Right then, there was a job to do. And two pairs of hands are better than one.

Sure, she had a nice figure. Long slender legs, strong firm hips and firmly rounded breasts, and I had eyes to see. But she'd been through hell and was needing help. It seems strange, I know, but right then I didn't think of her as a woman at all.

It took three or four hours to get her cleaned up, and although I used every drop of gasoline in the cans, she still wasn't thoroughly clean. But she was cleaned up sufficient to last until she had time to get down to a hot bath with plenty of good soap.

I swabbed the tar-marks off my clothes with the remaining drips from a can and cleaned my hands. Both of us smelled like a gas-station. I stripped off my shirt and pants, which were now dry. I kept on my undershorts. I jerked my head toward the river. 'Let's get washed up,' I said. 'We'll explode if we have to inhale this gas much longer.'

As we waded into the water she stumbled. She held out a hand toward me and automatically I held it. 'Don't go too deep,' she said. 'I can't swim.'

'Don't worry,' I said. 'I'll fish you out again.'

We wallowed around in the water for some time. It was cool and pleasant, washing away the fumes of gasoline and perspiration.

We climbed out of the river a little further along, where the bank was not plastered with tar scrapings and gasoline-soaked wads of cotton-waste. The sun was going down now, but it still had plenty of strength. We stretched out on the soft green bank with the sun beating down on us, drying us through and through.

'Feel better now?' I asked.

She was lying on her belly with her chin resting on her hands. 'Much better,' she said.

'You've had a tough time.'

'I guess I deserved it,' she said quietly.

I was lying on my back with my eyes closed. The sun was beating down on my chest. I couldn't see her face. I said: 'It took a lotta guts to stand up in court that way.'

'Not really,' she said. 'I couldn't let them lynch Robson, could I?'

'They might have killed you!'

I sensed her shudder of horror. 'It was dreadful,' she said. 'I knew there'd be an outcry. But I didn't think it would be that way. I thought I'd be shunned. I didn't think it would come to that.'

'Maybe it wouldn't have,' I said, 'but the crowd was set for a lynching. When they couldn't have that, they wanted something else to satisfy them.'

Her voice was suddenly anxious. 'They didn't get hold of Robson, did they?'

'No. The Sheriff got him out over the State line. He's safe enough.'

She breathed a sigh of relief. 'That's something to be thankful for,' she said.

I still wasn't looking at her. 'I guess you must like that guy an awful lot?'

'Like him?' There was surprise in her voice.

'Well, the way you stuck your neck out for him. I guess a dame has to be real nuts about a guy to do a thing like that.'

'You've got the wrong idea, too,' she said wearily. 'Robson didn't mean anything to me. Not that way. He was just sick. He was by himself. I knew he was sick, and that night I cooked some food for him and took it along. He was more sick than I'd thought. He was running a temperature. He was so bad I stopped with him all night.'

I turned my head and looked at her. Her green eyes stared back levelly. I cleared my throat and said huskily, 'You mean to tell me, all that happened in Robson's shack was that you nursed him while he was sick?'

'That's all,' she said quietly.

'You must be crazy,' I said. 'You know what the judge thought. You know what the jury thought. You know what that crowd outside thought. Why didn't you put them wise? Why didn't you make it clear you were just nursing the guy?

Her lips twisted in a bitter smile. 'D'you think it would have made any difference had I told them? Do you think they would have regarded that as anything more than a weak excuse?'

I thought it over. I thought of the jury and I thought of the judge. I thought of that blind, unreasoning crowd waiting outside like vultures. 'I guess not,' I said. 'I guess not.'

'You believe me, don't you?'

'Sounds reasonable to me.'

'You're a reasonable kinda fella,' she said simply. 'You come from the North. But down South, folks aren't reasonable. Not when it comes to dealing with coloured people.'

The sun dipped a little until part of it was cut off by the branches of a high tree.

'The question is,' I said, 'what are we going to do with you?'

'That's one of the things that's worrying me.'

'You can't go back.'

'I can't go back, yet everything I've got is tied up in Menton.'

'Property?'

She nodded. 'My house and the property my parents left me.'

'It's not so difficult,' I said. 'Find somewhere to stay for a time. Get your lawyer to sell out for you. You can do everything by post. No need to go back to Menton ever!'

'The question is,' she said soberly, 'where am I going to stay now? I've no money, nowhere to go …' Her voice dropped to a whisper. 'Not even clothes to wear.'

'Don't worry,' I said. 'We'll think of something.'

'You're so kind,' she said softly. 'I don't know what I'd have done without you.'

I turned over on my side until I was facing her. Her eyes were narrowed and her green pupils seemed to glow. I looked straight at her. 'I was pleased to help,' I told her.

'But you risked so much, and there's all this mess … and …'

'There was something about you I liked right from the first moment I saw you,' I confessed.

The green eyes seemed to grow even softer. 'And I was rude to you, wasn't I?'

'And when you were sitting there in the court, proud and defiant, giving evidence … well, I guess I thought you were just about the bravest girl I've ever seen.'

'And you've done so much,' she said. 'Got me away from those dreadful people, saved me when I wanted to drown myself, helped me clean off that dreadful mess …'

'You've a nice name, Virginia,' I said.

'You think so? Most folks think it's too long.'

'I like you, too.'

Her eyelids narrowed a fraction more, and her green eyes glowed slumberously. 'I guess I like you, too,' she said softly.

The sun dipped lower behind the trees. She pushed herself up into a sitting position and looked around. 'Oughtn't we to be going, doing something?'

'Yeah, I guess so,' I said. I sat up. 'Can't stop here much longer. It's getting dark.' I looked at her approvingly, searchingly. Her green eyes glowed, and then quite suddenly she blushed. She crossed her arms over her taut breasts and turned sideways to me. Her face was turned away from me shyly.

'Haven't you got something I can wear? I'm ... I'm ... cold.'

Since I'd got her away from the mob, this was the first time she'd realised her nakedness.

I guess she realised it just about the time she began to regard me as a man instead of just a good Samaritan.

After figuring all the angles, we decided the best thing was for Virginia to return to Chicago with me.

By driving real hard and all through the night, I reckoned to make Chicago during the early hours of the morning.

Virginia wrapped herself up in a blanket, and as soon as I got the car back onto the road, I put my foot down as far as it would go and held it there. I didn't risk stopping for something to eat until it was dark. Then I drew up well past a roadside café and walked back. I got sandwiches and a coupla cans of coffee.

We were both pretty hungry. We sat in the back of the car and ate ravenously. I had a bottle of rye under the dashboard. We both added a couple of shots of that toward warming up the coffee. Then I got back into the driving seat and Virginia curled up on the back seat.

As we drove along she talked, telling me about her life in Menton. It couldn't have been a very exciting life. Supervising the gardening, baking cakes for church socials, sitting on the front porch during the afternoon reading, and attending the Saturday night Bridge Club.

She yawned once or twice while she was talking, and I

wasn't surprised when her voice trailed away and she drifted into sleep. I let her sleep. After what she had been through, she needed a good rest.

I kept my foot down on the accelerator and roared on into the darkness of the night. As the hours passed, so the traffic became sparser. After a while it was like I was the only man in the world, racing along a black ribbon of road that vanished at the point where my headlights could reach no further. And as I drove I began to think about where I was taking Virginia. I was taking her to Cora Reid's nightclub. It was a swell joint on Blue Island Avenue, called the Two Spot.

Just why it was called the Two Spot, nobody knew, not that it mattered. A nightclub by any other name charged just as much.

7

It may seem strange that I was taking Virginia to a night club. But I had my reasons. Cora Reid owed me a debt of gratitude. I reckoned this was her chance to pay off. And, as I drove through the long night, my mind travelled back in time, recalling how I'd first met Cora Reid.

It had been three years before. Reporters get their noses into everything. As soon as it was known that a new nightclub was opening up on Blue Island Avenue, I was there, poking my nose in.

It was called the Two Spot before Cora took it over. A dull, lifeless place, run by a Pole so far gone in fatness he couldn't walk. Anytime you could see him squatting in the pay-box, his slit eyes almost concealed by bulging layers of fat. Nobody ever saw him away from that pay-box, and rumour had it he lived there day and night.

The shutters went up on the Two Spot and the place stayed shut for almost three months. During that time, builders and painters could be seen going in and out carrying long ladders, paint-pots and plaster. When Cora Reid opened the Two Spot again, she gave plenty of advance notice to the papers. She got good publicity, too. There wasn't a guy in Chicago who could read, who didn't know the day the Two Spot was going to open.

And, of course, I was there the opening night.

But starting off a nightclub requires more than mere

publicity. Folks are conservative by nature. They patronise their old haunts regularly, feeling at home in familiar surroundings. It takes something much more than a mere statement in the newssheet, that a new nightclub has opened, to bring the customers flocking to see the joint.

The Two Spot had been completely transformed. Thick carpets; soft lights; tremendous chandeliers; sleek, efficient waiters in dinner jackets; a newly-laid dancefloor; and a coloured band playing with sweaty enthusiasm.

It was a fine set-up. The only thing lacking was the customers. The joint was built to hold about two hundred. Instead there was about twenty diners there, talking in hushed voices and very conscious that they were in a wilderness.

I checked in my coat at the cloakroom and headed for the basement floor. A head-waiter greeted me with a pleasant smile, but disappointment tugged at the corner of his mouth. 'I'm sorry, sir,' he said. 'Evening dress only.'

'That's okay,' I said. 'I'm not staying. Just taking a drink at the bar.'

Again disappointment tugged at the corner of his mouth. 'Only diners may drink at the bar.'

I pulled out my press card. 'Just looking around,' I said.

'That's different,' he said.

It was a nice bar set up at the back of the nightclub. Clean as a new pin and glittering like a new toy. The crisp, white-coated bartender polished the gleaming counter, arched one eyebrow enquiringly.

'Highball,' I grunted.

He set it down in front of me on a cork disc. The band was playing a slow, languorous blues and the lights were lowered, while spotlights shone on the dancefloor. But nobody danced. Nobody wanted to go out there and dance a solo.

A medium-sized guy with hair parted in the middle and a toothbrush moustache eased himself alongside me and snapped his fingers. Without looking, the bartender mixed a drink and put it in front of him. I sensed he was standing there looking at me. I also sensed that he was swaying almost imperceptibly.

He patted his side pocket and then his breast pocket. The breast pocket produced results. He dived his hand down inside and came up with a slim, silver cigarette case. He opened it slowly, stared at the contents thoughtfully, and then carefully chose a cigarette. He got the cigarette halfway to his lips as he said:

'Got a light, pal?'

I'd been expecting that. I had my cigarette-lighter half out before he spoke. I struck it for him, and as he leaned toward the flame, he extended his cigarette case. I took one, lit it and puffed smoke thoughtfully into his face.

He stared back. His eyes were wide and blue. Just a little bit too wide. They were the mirror of his brain, reflecting hazed thoughts. He wasn't drunk, but he was a long way from being stone-cold sober.

'Ben Hilton,' he introduced himself.

'Julius Caesar,' I replied.

He wagged his forefinger at me. 'You're a reporter,' he said.

I looked around slowly. I didn't see any smoke-signals and I couldn't hear any jungle drums beating out a message. 'Watch out you don't tread on your ears,' I said.

He stroked one ear thoughtfully. 'They told me,' he explained. 'I'm the manager here.'

I looked him over with fresh interest. 'You're the guy that's been flooding newspaper offices with opening announcements.'

He beamed and nodded his head. He swayed ever so slightly as he put his glass to his lips and tilted his head. He looked like a guy who'd been tippling so long he couldn't straighten his elbow.

'How long are you reckoning on staying open?'

It was his turn to glance around at the almost deserted nightclub. The smile slipped from his face and a sad look came into his eyes. 'We can stand this maybe two weeks,' he said. 'We can't stand it longer than that. Most of the dough went into buying the place and getting it ready.'

'It was an ambitious idea,' I said. 'But this is a big town. Things often get unstuck.'

He shook his head sorrowfully. 'I had great hopes,' he said. 'I'd hate to see it go up in smoke.'

'You got an interest in the joint?'

He considered the question 'Well, I guess I have. But not a financial interest. I get my salary, win or lose. But I'd sure hate to see Cora lose out.'

'Cora?'

He nodded glumly. 'Cora Reid. This is her joint, her idea. She put up the dough.'

'Seems like I haven't heard about her.'

'She likes to keep in the background.' He snapped his fingers for another drink, and the bartender looked at me enquiringly. I nodded.

'She's the one with the ideas and the initiative. She's put everything she's got into this,' he went on.

'Looks like a tough break for her.'

'Yeah,' he said moodily. 'If there was only some way of whipping up the customers ...'

He broke off, looked over my shoulder and straightened himself up. His eyes softened and he took on the appearance of a devoted spaniel. 'Hello, Cora,' he said. 'Going to have a drink?'

I turned around so I could get a good look at her. She was tall and lissom, wearing a sheath-like black evening gown. It was a backless gown and very nearly frontless. The creamy-white swell of her breasts hit me right in the eyes, and the valley between them was deep, exotic and tantalisingly shadowy. There wasn't anything I could see to support the dress, and I had the feeling it was gonna slip any minute. I daren't look away in case it did.

Ben Hilton cleared his throat and said loudly, 'This gentleman's a reporter, Cora. He's from the *Chronicle*.'

'Indeed!' Her voice was husky and controlled, and although she spoke only one word, she seemed to pack into it a mocking, contemptuous note. I took a chance on the dress slipping and raised my eyes. Jeepers, she was beautiful. Beautiful like a Greek goddess; and somehow she seemed just about as remote.

And she seemed to have the stateliness of a queen. Her smooth, arched eyebrows were imperturbable and her eyes were cool, grey and hard as they probed me.

'Janson,' I murmured, feeling a little breathless. 'Hank Janson.'

'Something worrying you?' she asked. She was deliberately mocking me. Her eyes watched me almost disdainfully. Those grey eyes seemed to probe deep into my brain, reading my thoughts. She knew what was worrying me: I was having a hard job keeping my eyes on her face instead of letting them slip down to the top of her dress.

'No,' I said. 'I guess you've got a nice place here. Kinda cosy.' I couldn't help it. My eyes flickered. And the dress hadn't slipped.

'We tried to make it nice,' she said. 'Ben's worked so hard, too.' Her eyes softened as they rested lightly on him for a moment. She shrugged her shoulders almost pathetically, and my eyes took time off to notice how white and soft her shoulders were. 'I had hoped that our first night would show good results.'

I picked up my drink and gazed into the bottom of the glass. 'It's tough getting a nightclub started up,' I said.

'Do you think it will be a success, Mr Janson?'

I still looked at the bottom of my glass. 'Take a look around,' I said.

She took a look around. That meant she turned her back to me. She had fair hair, upswept in the Victorian style, so that it showed the softness of her neck as it blended into her shoulders. Her back was bare right down to her hips, and I was so close to her I could see the fine, silvery down in the hollow of her spine.

'How many?' I asked.

'Twenty,' she counted.

'Tonight's opening night,' I pointed out. 'There'll be even fewer tomorrow.' I wanted to wet my finger and rub it down her back just to see her reaction.

She turned back to me just in time. I already had my

forefinger in my mouth. It's funny how sometimes you give way to a childish impulse.

'Ben's worked so hard to get publicity,' she said sadly.

My eyes flicked to the neckline, tried to probe the mystery of that shadowy valley. Her skin was soft and milk-white, and again I got that irresistible impulse to touch.

'Mr Janson,' she said in a cool, clear voice, 'haven't you any more intelligence than to want to ogle like a schoolboy?'

I cleared my throat, stammered, shuffled my feet, and my hands seemed awkward and about forty times their normal size. I didn't know what to do with them. I didn't know what to do with myself. She made me feel like a reprimanded small boy.

'Well?' she asked coolly, her grey eyes indifferent and without emotion. 'Haven't you anything to say?'

'Sure I have,' I said. I'd gathered my resources together. 'I'm a human being, see. What's more, I'm a man! Furthermore, you're a dame. A beautiful dame. And you're wearing the kinda dress that shows me just how beautiful you are. That does things, lady. I'd be a liar if I said it didn't. You can't kick a fella's pants because he's human.'

The grey eyes were still cool and indifferent. But there was a suggestion of contempt curling the corners of her lips as she said, 'How childish.'

Ben cleared his throat loudly and said, 'How about a drink, Cora?'

'No, thank you, Ben,' she said softly. Her voice was somehow different when she spoke to him. Her grey eyes became amused and ironical. 'Perhaps you can find Mr Jansen some photographs. Art studies. He could have some pleasant evenings at home studying them.'

'Perhaps you'd like to be put across my knee and spanked,' I said, with an ugly note in my voice.

Ben's hand rested lightly on my shoulder, pressing warningly, restraining me. Cora laughed. A low, soft laugh.

'Please, Mr Janson,' she chided. 'Don't take your hair down in public.'

'Don't rib him, Cora,' pleaded Ben. 'He's just not used to it.

Besides, he's a reporter.'

Her eyebrows arched a fraction of an inch. 'Of course,' she said. 'You're a reporter. We must be nice to you, mustn't we?'

'Go jump in the lake,' I growled.

'How about a drink, Cora?' asked Ben, pacifically.

'Not now,' she said. 'I'll be down later.' The grey eyes mocked me. 'I hope you'll become a regular customer, Mr Janson.'

I grunted.

Ben had another drink lined up for me almost as soon as she'd left us. He swallowed half of his with evident satisfaction, gently ran his tongue over his lips and said: 'She's difficult to understand.'

'You understand her?'

'I ought to. I was her manager at a nightclub in Los Angeles for three years before we came here.'

'Cute kid!' I breathed hard.

'She's all right when you know her. A real smart kid.'

I looked him over with new interest. 'You haven't any interest in this club?'

'She's the boss,' he said. 'Her money, her ideas.'

I leered at him artfully. 'And apart from that, you've got no interest?' I allowed a wicked, suggestive note to enter my voice. 'She's got some figure.'

He stared at me unwinkingly. 'You've got it wrong, fella. There ain't anything like that between me and Cora.'

I looked him over slowly. 'Who's kidding?'

He shook his head gently. 'She's a queer kid,' he said. 'You saw the way she was with you. That's the way she is with everybody. Three years I've known her, and she hasn't taken a tumble once. Men slide off her like water off a duck's back. I've seen them try it, time and again. And I guess there wasn't one who even made her flicker an eyelash.'

'How about you?' I asked. 'You seem to have been around.'

He shrugged his shoulders. 'I'm human, too, ain't I?' he asked. He spread his hands in a gesture of futileness. 'Can't even get to first base. A fella couldn't help trying. It just wouldn't be natural not to try. But she's got ways of chilling off a guy that would create a revolution in the quick-freezing industry.'

'There's nothing funny about her, is there?'

His eyes were soft and thoughtful now. 'She's a grand kid,' he said. 'I guess I'd do almost anything for her. But she just doesn't seem to realise a fella's human. Maybe I'm just not the fella. Maybe, sometime a fella will come along who'll get her interested.' He bent his elbow and finished off his drink. He banged the glass back on the counter. 'I'm just hoping not,' he said.

'There's just one thing you ought to remember about dames,' I told him. 'They're just like stones. When they want, they can be hard and unfeeling.'

He smiled, wryly. 'Don't I know it.'

I finished my drink and stood up. 'There's one other thing to remember,' I said. 'Stone, even the hardest stone, is worn away by steadily dripping water.'

He snapped his fingers for another drink, and I left him with a thoughtful look on his face, chewing over what I'd just said.

I looked in there a coupla nights later and had another drink with Ben and Cora. Like I thought, folks weren't coming back after the opening night. The band was playing for two old business guys who kept looking around with disgruntled expressions on their faces that seemed to say that, despite everything, they'd have their meal before they cleared out.

Ben was despondent and Cora was quiet and thoughtful. She hadn't even put on an evening gown. She was wearing a smartly-tailored costume and a white cross-over blouse.

There was something about Cora. She fascinated me, intrigued me. Maybe it was because I hadn't met a girl quite like her before. Maybe it was because I sensed her insensibility as a woman and accepted it as a challenge to my vanity.

I dropped in there several nights after that, and every time, Cora was there. But business was bad. Very bad. Toward the end of the week, Cora confessed she couldn't stand another week like it. She'd be finished. Dead broke.

I thought about her situation for a coupla days, turning over in my mind all kinds of projects. Finally I got one idea that seemed to be a real humdinger.

When I got to the bar that night, Ben was standing there bending his elbow as usual.

'Where's Cora?'

'She's not too well today,' he said. 'Got a headache. She's stopped upstairs.'

'I wanna see her,' I said. 'I've got an idea that might put the Two Spot on the map. Think she'll be well enough to talk it over?'

'You wouldn't like to tell me?'

'I'd sooner discuss it with her.'

'I'll go and see,' he said.

He came back in five minutes. 'She'd like you to go up,' he said.

'Which way?'

'I'll show you.'

He took me through a side door and up some thickly-carpeted stairs. At the top was a long corridor. He stopped at the third door along and knocked.

When she called out for him to enter, he opened the door, stood to one side and ushered me in. He closed the door softly behind me, and Cora said in that husky voice of hers, 'Sit down, Hank.'

I swallowed hard and my mouth went dry. It was her bedroom. It was tastefully and daintily furnished, and she'd obviously been in bed. The sheets were still pulled back, and I could see the indentation her body had made. She was sitting up in a chair, wearing a light blue negligee, and her tiny bare feet were thrust into furry blue mules.

I eased myself down into a chair opposite her and moistened my lips. 'I didn't want to bother you if you're not well,' I said. 'But I've got something that might interest you.'

'It's nice of you to come,' she said. 'I'm quite all right now. I rested most of the day. It seemed hardly worthwhile to get up so late.'

'You're sure I'm not disturbing you?'

She chuckled. That low, husky chuckle. 'I'm as fit as a fiddle.'

I got out my cigarette case and then began to put it back again. 'That's all right,' she said quickly. 'Smoke your head off. I don't mind. And get yourself a drink. Just behind you.'

While I mixed the drink I said, 'The way things are going you'll be finished in a week's time.'

'I'm afraid so.' Her husky voice was forlorn.

'Things ain't gonna get better the way they are,' I said. 'They're gonna get worse. Why just sit around for another week waiting for the big bangs? Why not be smart? Splash the dough you're saving to cover next week's expenses and try to save everything.'

I turned away from the sideboard, carrying our drinks. She changed her position in the chair, and crossed her legs. Her negligee fell open, and I could see her cool flesh gleaming through the transparent nightgown she was wearing beneath it.

I sat down opposite her and looked at her legs. They were long and shapely, and the nightdress was so filmy I could see the dimples in her knees.

'I'm not interrupting you?' she said softly.

I cleared my throat and switched my mind back to business. 'This is the idea,' I said. 'You send an invitation to Joe Burke to bring a dozen of his pals along on Friday night to dine on the house. Then pray like hell he'll accept the invitation.'

'And who is Joe Burke?'

'You'll have to take my word for it,' I said. 'He's an up-and-coming heavyweight champion. Pretty soon he'll be right at the top.'

'And?' she asked. The eyebrows were arched, the grey eyes cool and clear, and she moved her legs slightly as she nestled into a more comfortable position. As she moved, her mule fell off, revealing one dainty bare foot.

'Allow me,' I said. I went down on one knee and picked up her mule. I took her ankle in one hand and gently eased the mule back onto her foot. The hem of the nightgown came down to her ankle. When I took her foot, my hand went just underneath the hem. I took a long while easing the mule into position, and thrilled at the touch of her cool leg.

As I got up, I was careless with my hand, and it brushed along her calf.

The cool grey eyes were indifferent. 'The heavyweight champion?'

'Yeah,' I said. I sat down, mopped my face with my handkerchief and reached for my drink.

'Well?'

'Yeah,' I said. 'About Joe Burke. You get him here, see? Then you've got to get yourself a cabaret turn, a dame.' My eyes flickered toward her knees and then back to her face. 'A cabaret turn that goes over.'

Her eyebrows raised even more. 'Meaning what?'

'A striptease dame,' I said. I stared at her levelly.

Momentarily, her eyes widened and grew hard. 'Just for your benefit?' There was a sarcastic inflection in her voice.

'You've gotta understand something.' I said. 'Striptease is what folks like. It's popular. Folks go places just to see it. Give the customers what they want and you've got no complaints.'

'So,' she said disdainfully. 'A striptease act.'

'More than that,' I said. 'You've got to get an artist with brains. You've got to get a dame who can do with a little publicity and who can act as well.'

'When do we get around to the idea?'

'If you'll only keep your trap shut I'll get around to it,' I said.

'How dare you …' she began.

'Shuddup,' I yelled. 'I'm talking.'

The grey eyes were startled, and her mouth made a little O of surprise.

'That's fine,' I said. 'Just stay that way.' I sure had startled her, talking that way. But before she had recovered from her surprise, I'd already plunged into the details of my plan. Her startled expression changed to one of interest. When I was through she asked:

'And will that get customers?'

'Lady,' I said, 'we won't be able to keep them away. I'll pass the news around. It'll be a front-page splash on every newspaper. They'll be queueing to see that dame.'

'And what about Joe Burke? Isn't it rather rough on him?'

My face hardened. 'Joe Burke got where he is today by playing dirty. Taking a dive when he was told to and knowing other guys were being paid to lay down in front of him. A guy of that character can't harm much.'

'It certainly sounds worth trying,' she said. 'But what about the other boxer?'

'That's my angle,' I said. 'You leave that to me. You'll have a job getting the cabaret artiste. You've got to pick the right girl, and she's gotta play her part, and she's gotta do it for dough. She won't do it for nothing.'

'I'll do it,' she said suddenly, impulsively. 'I'll do it, even if it doesn't work out. Things can't be any worse than they are now.'

'Just what I've been saying,' I said. I finished my drink, looked at her knees, and asked, 'Another drink?'

'Help yourself. I've had enough.'

I poured myself another drink. But I didn't sit down. I went and stood alongside her, close to her. She had to lean her head back to look up into my face. I said seriously: 'I've not known you long, Cora. Does it surprise you to know I like you a helluva lot?'

'No,' she said soberly. Her eyes were cool and grey. She took my statement matter-of-fact, as though it happened every day.

'I guess you thought it strange, the way I've been coming around.'

'Not particularly,' she said calmly. 'Lots of fellas have done that.'

'Okay,' I said gruffly. 'Well, you've got lots of fellas on the hook. But that doesn't mean to say I can't try, does it?'

'Try what, Hank?' she asked quietly.

I swallowed my drink, put the glass on a glass-topped table and stood squarely in front of her. 'If that's what you're thinking, you're wrong,' I said. 'I haven't tried anything, and I'm not going to. Can't you see, I'm just trying to tell you that I like you more ... for ... well, I guess just for yourself.'

She said, 'Oh,' softly, and breathed out slowly. The cool grey eyes seemed just a little softer now. Then she sighed. 'I'm sorry, Hank,' she said. 'It wouldn't work out. It couldn't.'

'Listen,' I said, thickly. 'I've been coming around seeing you. I've been thinking about you at night, the sound of your voice, remembering your eyes. You've been growing on me more and more every day since I first saw you. That kinda thing doesn't happen for nothing.'

She shook her head slowly. 'It's no good Hank,' she said. 'It's no good. It wouldn't work out.'

'It would,' I insisted. 'If you wanted. If you wanted and I wanted, nothing could stop it.'

She looked away from me. Her head was slightly bowed but her voice was firm. 'It's no good, Hank. It wouldn't work out. Please don't mention it anymore.'

'You haven't got the guts to try,' I said.

She looked back at me then, and this time her grey eyes were really soft. 'I do like you, Hank. It's been the same with me. I've been thinking of you, too.'

'Don't let's rush things,' I said. 'Let them have their head. Maybe it will work out just fine and dandy.'

I saw the softness in her eyes change to thoughtfulness. She got up slowly as she said: 'You've got to see it the way it is. It's no use, Hank. It's no use.'

'Jeepers,' I pleaded. 'Haven't you got any feeling?'

She looked at me steadily. 'All right, Hank,' she said. 'You'll have to have it the hard way. You've got to realise what you're up against.'

I looked at her suspiciously. 'What are you getting at?'

'You'll see,' she said. She untied the girdle of her negligee and shrugged out of it. Her milk-white skin shimmered beneath the transparent gossamer of her nightdress like an elusive wisp of some maddening scent. I suddenly found I'd lost my breath. I kinda gasped, and there was a pain deep down inside me, a sharp pain that was almost ecstasy.

She stood there facing me squarely, her calm grey eyes fixed on my face and her hands limp at her sides. The low-cut bodice revealed most of her breasts, and the table-lamp behind her sent its rays streaming through the nightgown so that her limbs stood out in stark relief.

'Cora,' I said harshly. 'You don't mean …?'

'I want you to know it's no good, Hank.'

I wanted to touch the soft whiteness of her skin, to feel its smooth texture beneath my fingers. What guy wouldn't have wanted that? But there was something strange and elusive about her. Something that held me back.

'You've got it wrong, Cora,' I said. 'It isn't just this. It's something more. I want you for yourself. Not just because I'm a man.'

Her beautiful face was white and set. Her grey eyes were still probing into me, cool and strangely hard.

'I want you to know the way it is, Hank,' she said. As she spoke, she slipped the slender straps of her nightgown down over her shoulders. There was nothing to hold it then. It shimmered as it slipped down her body and around her feet, and she stood there, poised and erect, like a beautiful goddess. I wanted her. I wanted her like hell. My knees were hot and trembling and I was panting. But still there was something about her. She was beautiful, divine like a goddess; but, like a goddess, she was something to be admired from a distance.

'Here I am, Hank,' she said softly. 'If you want me.'

'Sure, I want you,' I said harshly. I passed my hand across my brow and it came away damp. 'But it's not just that way, Cora. I'm not rushing you into a clinch.'

'You've got to know what you're up against, Hank,' she said.

'I don't understand,' I said desperately. I ran my fingers through my hair. 'This is all so crazy.'

'Is it? What's the matter, Hank? Don't you want me? I'm here if you do.'

Well, of course I wanted her. I took her in two quick strides. My arms encircled her, and I crushed her hard against me while my lips found hers and savaged them. I was overpowered by the knowledge of her nakedness. I was hot and trembling, my senses swimming with desire, and the smell of jasmine was in my nostrils like a soft scent carried on a cool breeze. For a moment I knew only a delirious ecstasy as I pulled her close to me, felt her soft skin beneath my fingers and tasted the cool sweetness of her lips. And then the hammering of my pulse died away as my hot blood began to cool. There was something. Her body was arched against mine. Her arms were around my neck. Her lips were pressed against mine.

But there was something.

I opened my eyes while I was kissing her and found her cool grey eyes staring at mine. There was no urgent desire in her expression. Only cool wonderment.

'Try, Hank,' she whispered desperately. 'Try.'

She arched her body against me and her fingers gripped me so tightly they bruised.

But there was something!

Her skin was cool and soft beneath my fingers. And she was cool, too. Did I say cool? She was ice cold. The pressure of her body against mine was forced. The pressure of her arms around my neck was deliberate. There was no warmth in her lips as she kissed, and my touch had no effect upon her. She kinda laid back in my arms with abandonment. 'Try, Hank,' she whispered urgently.

I didn't have to try, because I wanted her. When I caressed her it was because of the desire burning inside me. But the desire died. It died quickly. It died even more quickly as I realised my embrace was of no significance to her.

After a time, she pushed herself away from me gently. 'You see the way it is,' she said simply.

'Yeah,' I said. I felt strange. I felt like a hungry man who loses his appetite when food is offered. 'Is it always this way?'

She began climbing back into her nightgown. Somehow she didn't disturb me anymore. One shoulder strap had broken, and as she tied it together, one taut cherry-tipped breast seemed to point at me. I was surprised I could admire the classical lines of her body without feeling deep emotion.

'Has it always been that way?' I repeated.

She got the strap back over her shoulder, and the white breast shimmered beneath transparent covering. 'Not always, Hank,' she said softly. 'It was just something that happened. After that I was never the same.'

'You don't feel … anything?'

'Nothing,' she said. 'Kissing or being loved just doesn't mean anything.'

'I'll have another drink,' I said.

I felt like hell. I mixed myself another drink and felt like hell all the time I was doing it. She was there, beautiful and desirable. But it meant nothing to her. And until it meant something to her, it could mean nothing to me.

I turned around and said softly: 'It doesn't make any difference, Cora. Things will change, perhaps. Perhaps in time it could be different.'

She was putting on her negligee. She shook her head slowly. 'It's no good, Hank,' she said. 'Can't you see that. I'm the way I am. And that isn't good enough.'

I eyed her steadily. 'That doesn't have to be the only reason I want you.'

She smiled then. It was the smile of a madonna. A strange, inscrutable smile that reflected the sum of woman's understanding throughout the ages. 'It wouldn't be the same without, Hank. It might not be everything, but it has a part, an important part.'

'What caused it?' I burst out. 'You said you'd tell me.'

Her face became hard. 'I'll tell you sometime,' she promised. 'Not now.' And then she smiled, squared her shoulders and said cheerfully: 'Let's discuss the plan a little more. We ought to settle all the details.'

'Give me time,' I said. 'You won't always be this way …'

She heaved a great sigh and managed to look as though her patience was exhausted. 'Don't be tiresome,' she said. 'I've shown you how useless it is. Must I go through all that again?'

'Maybe we can do it different next time.'

A shadow of a smile flickered across her face. Then her face became set and hard again. 'For heaven's sake, Hank,' she said. 'You're wearing me out. If you can't drop the subject, I'll have to ask you to leave.'

I looked at her with one eyebrow raised. She stared back. Her eyes were hard and grey. She meant what she said.

I swallowed, breathed hard and said: 'About Joe Burke.'

'You'll have to let me have his address,' she said.

8

As soon as I knew Joe Burke had accepted Cora's invitation, I telephoned a young fella named John Ganton. He was an up-and-coming young boxer, full of promise but finding it difficult to get places on account of his honesty. The guys who rigged the fight game liked to be sure their boys would take a dive when they were told. John Ganton wasn't the boy to take orders. As a result he found it heavy going.

'How would you like a match with Joe Burke?' I asked.

'I'd give my ears for it,' he said. 'I've been trying to get a match with him for months. The top boys are too clever. They steer away.'

'Maybe the issue can be forced,' I mused.

'Yeah?'

'It's up to you,' I told him. 'Here's the angle.'

I told him what I had in mind and why I was doing it, and he accepted the suggestion right away. I knew he would. The only other thing then was the publicity.

Reporters are only fellas doing a job of work. The easier they can get a story, the better they like it. I carefully selected the fellas I knew working on the other papers and told them what I aimed to do. They were straight guys. They liked the idea. They liked it as much as anything because it was an easy story to get.

Everything was well planned. When Joe Burke and his dozen 'free' guests went to the Two Spot and were shown to a table near the dancefloor, half-a-dozen newsboys were packed away out of sight with their cameras handy.

There were a few other customers around when John Ganton arrived. I winked at the head waiter, who had been carefully instructed on what to do, and he led John Ganton across to the table next to Joe Burke.

Joe Burke knew Ganton. His lip curled and he gave a sullen nod of acknowledgement. It was no less sullen than the nod Johnny returned.

The head waiter was playing his part. He kept Joe Burke's table lavishly supplied with champagne and food. Joe Burke's party became quite noisy. In fact, it was probably the first time that the Two Spot, under the management of Ben Hilton, had shown any signs of festivity.

The stage was well set by the time the cabaret act began. And just so it shouldn't be so obvious, there were three cabaret turns. The first was a ventriloquist, the second a magician, and the third was the striptease dame.

She had an act all of her own. She did it well, too. She came on wearing a white blouse and a black pleated skirt and singing a song about love. She was a pretty dame with big eyes and a knack of writhing her hips. She kept singing at Joe Burke and rolling her eyes, and pretty soon he turned around so he could sit facing her. She played back. She twitched her hips at him provokingly, and a greasy smirk spread across his features. When the song was through, all lights went out except one spotlight playing on the centre of the dancefloor. Somebody put a small stool under the spotlight and the dame sat on the stool with her skirt up over her knees. She began to sing another song about a fella and a girl.

It was a spicy, sexy song, and the dame did actions in accordance with the words.

The first words of the song were about a dame taking off her stockings. The dame did that very well. She wore high-heeled shoes and black stockings. She was squarely facing Joe Burke when she pulled up her skirt, showing a white froth of underclothes, among which she fumbled to unclip her stockings from the suspender.

That dame sure knew her stuff. She seemed to be all slim, provoking legs, as she rolled her stockings down around her ankles, and the words of her song sent Burke and his friends into fits of laughter.

I was watching Burke most of the time. I could see he was getting good and het up, and to my satisfaction, the waiter was carrying out his instructions and continually filling his glass with champagne.

The dame went on with her act. Barefoot now, she danced and kicked high. Then she undid the top button of her blouse and fumbled inside. It was the old stunt of a fella taking off his shirt without removing his coat, brought up to date. She fumbled around inside her blouse, arched her body, wriggled prettily and finally drew out her brassiere, which she'd worked off. There was a gale of laughter as this action fitted in so aptly with the words of the song. And then a burst of applause.

The dame smiled her appreciation, danced with swaying hips to Joe Burke, and with a swift movement festooned his neck with the brassiere. That caused more laughter.

She was going on with her act. The striptease became more apparent. Dancing sensuously the whole time, she used the flare of her skirt as a cover as she stripped ingeniously. Spinning so that her pleated skirt flared out horizontally from her hips to reveal white briefs, she displayed her hands, showing them empty. She stopped suddenly, faced Burke and, standing with feet together, wriggled her body. She smiled at him cheekily as she fumbled behind her, up and under her skirt. Then slowly she turned in a full circle, all the time keeping her fumbling on the side farthest from Burke. When she'd completed a full turn, she whipped from beneath the skirt her girdle. She was too quick for Burke. She looped it around his neck and danced away before he realised what had happened.

That caused much more laughter, and Joe Burke flourished the girdle like it was a flag. 'It's still warm,' he chuckled loudly.

The dame was spinning again now, her skirt flaring out horizontally. Her white briefs fitted snug and tight.

Again she stood near Joe Burke, looking at him cheekily.

With legs partly astride she wriggled her body. Burke was grinning all over his face. The girl was narrowing her eyes at him, raising her hands up level with her ears as she sucked in her belly, wriggled her hips sensuously and panted slightly.

Nobody caught on at first to what she was doing. There was a look of concentration on her face as her belly and thighs twisted and jerked. And then suddenly everybody understood; something white appeared at the hem of her skirt and hovered for a moment before it slipped down her calves to the ground. The dame stepped out of her white briefs, and with a deft kick lifted them in an arc through the air so they fell on Burke's lap.

She danced swiftly after that. She didn't let the skirt flare quite so high. But it flared high enough to suggest that the briefs musta been all she was wearing. And then came the final part of her act.

The newsboys had sensed the climax was coming. They were edging up close now. Nobody took any notice of them in the gloom of the nightclub. Only the spotlighted dancefloor invited attention.

The girl was standing near Joe Burke again. She undid the buttons of her blouse all the way down the front and slipped the blouse off her shoulder. Beneath it she wore a slip. A beautifully-made slip that encased her breasts exactly. Joe Burke's tongue was almost hanging out.

And then she started her body movements again. It seemed to be much more difficult this time, because the skirt fitted tightly. For the first few moments it looked like she was making no progress. And then, suddenly, amazingly, the controlled movements of her body brought the skirt lower and lower over her hips. It was hard work. The dame's forehead was glistening with perspiration and her belly and hips were rolling and contracting sinuously, like a snake rippling through grass.

The skirt came lower and lower over her hips, slipped down until it was round her thighs, and then the movements of her thigh muscles caused it to fall to the ground. She stepped out of the skirt and stood there smiling, acknowledging the burst of applause. I guess the applause was as much for the way she looked now as for her performance. That slip was beautifully tailored. It fitted her body like it was skin. The hem of the slip was just low enough! And what made it more interesting was, you could tell right away it was the only garment she wore. She wasn't wearing a stitch beneath it.

Joe Burke was applauding vigorously. The brassiere was still looped around his neck and the white briefs and girdle were on his lap. She smiled and took a coupla steps toward him with hands outstretched for her garments. As she did so she seemed to slip. She plunged toward him. Automatically Joe Burke reached out to save her. She sprawled into his lap.

Everything happened so quickly it was difficult for anybody to know exactly what happened. I knew, because I'd planned what was going to happen.

By the time the girl got to her feet again, the strap of her slip had broken. Her slip dangled down, exposing one firm pointed breast, and the girl flared at Burke, calling him names and looking the picture of outraged virginity. Except, of course, that she made no attempt to cover the exposed breast. When she slapped Joe Burke's face he was surprised outta his life. His mouth was a great O of surprise. He was so surprised that he didn't even notice the flashes as the newsboys got their photos.

But that wasn't all. Johnny Ganton was sitting at the next table. In a coupla strides he was across the room and jerked Burke out of his chair. He hung one on his chin that sent him spinning a coupla yards away.

The newsboys got a lotta shots. A lotta good shots. They showed Johnny and Burke slugging it out, and all of them seemed to manage to get into the background the cabaret artist wearing just the slip, and only half of it at that.

It was in all the papers the next day. It made a front-page spread. It got written up just the way I wanted it. Headlines announced Joe Burke had been worked to a frenzy by a striptease girl in a nightclub. Much speculation was made as to the desirability of this girl. Much speculation was made as to the possibility of Johnny Ganton and Joe Burke fighting it out in the ring now that Burke had got a licking in a nightclub fight.

There was lots of angles to be played up, and all of them were news angles. And whatever angle was used was all publicity for the Two Spot.

The public is a queer animal. The scene of a murder will fascinate people so much that, years after, they will loiter near the house and point and gloat. 'He was murdered here.'

We hit the jackpot with this news story. Lots of folks came to the Two Spot to see the dancer who had been almost devirginised in public by Burke. Many came to see the place where the incident had taken place. Many came to see the spot on which Johnny Ganton and Burke had slugged it out. And many others came just in the hope it would happen all over again.

The Two Spot was made overnight. Johnny Ganton got his match with Burke and Cora signed the striptease artist on for a long contract. It worked out swell for everybody except Burke, and he didn't matter anyway.

There was one other guy who was really pleased. That was Ben Hilton. He just couldn't thank me enough. That made me feel mean. He thanked me, whereas all I'd been doing was trying to get in well with Cora.

I knew how Ben would hate that, if I succeeded.

9

All of that had happened a long while ago. And the intervening years had seen many changes in the Two Spot. It was now one of the best money-spinners and the most frequented of the many nightclubs that Chicago boasted. Cora had gone up in the world. She'd developed the nightclub, taken over the property next door and set up furnished suites above the club, which brought in a nice side income as well as enabling her to live rent free.

That development had taken a lotta hard work, and Cora and Ben Hilton had every right to be proud of their achievement. Yeah, Cora had made out all right. But, even so, she musta realised that if it hadn't been for my intervention, things might not have turned out so well after all.

There was no denying that Cora owed me something. And when the nightclub had become firmly established, Cora had tried to square things. But I hadn't want dough. I'd done it because I like giving folks a helping hand when I can, and ... well ... I guess I kinda liked Cora at that.

I'd hung around the Two Spot a lot at first. She'd had that kinda effect upon me. She still looked good to me. She'd look good to any guy with an eye for a dame's curves, I guess. But time always changes things. She was a dame who sent my temperature up to fever-pitch at close quarters. But when it was closer than close quarters, she chilled me off quicker than a coupla days in the cold-storage vault.

I got used to seeing Cora around, knowing she was just about the prettiest piece of goods that ever wore lace underwear, yet realising what she'd told me was true. It just wouldn't work out. It never could have worked out. Even if a dame isn't warm and cuddly all the time, she just has got to be warm and cuddly some of the time.

Cora just wasn't warm and cuddly any of the time.

So, as time drifted on, my visits to the Two Spot became less frequent. I liked Cora. Sure, I liked Ben Hilton, too. But seeing them occasionally was sufficient to keep the friendship warm.

But Cora still had an obligation to me. And right now it seemed like she was gonna get a chance to pay me back. She was a goodhearted dame and reliable.

I had a dame on my hands, naked as the day she was born and with nowhere to go. Cora's joint was the first place I thought of.

I drove furiously. I drove through the night with my headlights cutting through the darkness like a sickle shearing through corn. My tyres skimmed the road and grew hot with friction. The engine throbbed into the long, long night, and I reached Chicago in the early hours of the morning.

I drove straight to the Two Spot. There was a private parking lot at the rear. I drove around back, switched off my lights and tucked the blanket even more closely around Virginia.

'Where are we?' she asked wearily.

'We're okay,' I said. 'We're with friends. Just hold on. I'll be back in no time.'

I fumbled my way through the rear entrance to the block and up the darkened stairs to the first floor. I knew where Cora's apartment was. I found the bell-push and leant my weight on it.

It took about five minutes for her to wake up and slip on a negligee. When she opened the door it had the night-chain in place.

She spoke through the crack of the door suspiciously.

'Who's that?' she demanded.

'Hank,' I said. 'You've got to let me in, Cora.'

'What a helluva time to come calling,' she grumbled. 'You go and take a jump in the lake.'

'Don't be dumb,' I said. 'This ain't a social call. This is urgent business.'

She let the door off the chain and closed the door behind me. 'What's so awful important?' she demanded angrily.

'I've gotta dame in the back of my car,' I said. 'She's stripped. Not a stitch on her. Nowhere to go. I want your help.'

Her eyes widened and her eyebrows arched. 'Dame in the back of the car? Stripped naked? What d'you want my help for? You seem to be doing all right by yourself.'

'She's in trouble,' I said. 'Real trouble. I wouldn't get you up this time of the night for fun. Can I bring the dame up here? I'll give you the lowdown later.'

Her eyes examined me carefully, considered and decided. 'Wait a minute,' she said. A few moments later she was back with an outdoor coat. She thrust it into my hands. 'Bring her up,' she said. 'I'll start brewing some coffee.'

I fumbled my way back to the car, helped Virginia into the coat, and then guided her upstairs to Cora's apartment. Nobody saw us. I closed the door behind me and ushered Virginia through into the living-room; I settled her in a divan and she huddled there, looking forlorn and miserable. My hair surgery hadn't been too efficient. Her hair looked just what it was: hacked about with a penknife.

Cora came in with a pot of coffee. She set it down on a small table and I made the introductions. The two dames watched each other warily, like a coupla tigers circling around, measuring each other up. I noticed then how Virginia's eyes seemed to glow greenly, and there was just the suggestion of an amused twist to the corners of Cora's mouth as she took in the jagged ends of Virginia's hair.

'I'm sorry about troubling you like this,' said Virginia. 'But it was Hank's idea. He said …'

'Quite all right, my dear,' interrupted Cora. She flashed me a smile. 'With Hank, one never knows what he's up to next.'

'There was nowhere else I could go, Cora,' I said. 'I guess it just had to be you.'

She shrugged her shoulders ruefully. 'Well, if it just had to be me, I guess it just had to be me. Don't stand there awkwardly like that, Hank. Sit down, pour yourself a cup of coffee and let's hear what all this is about.'

I sat down and sipped appreciatively at the coffee. After all that driving I felt tired. Virginia must have felt like hell. You could see the infinite weariness in her eyes and in the way she slumped limply on the divan.

'You can settle back, Cora,' I said. 'It's gonna take a long time to tell.'

I left out nothing. I told Cora everything that had happened. I had my reasons. It's much more difficult to raise pity in a woman about another woman, than it is to arouse a man's pity. That's why I went into the details.

I guess it shocked Cora. She was the kinda dame who had enough imagination to figure out what it would be like if she had to undergo that experience.

By the time I was through telling the story, Virginia, completely exhausted, had fallen asleep. Cora kept flicking little sidelong glances of pity at her.

'I had to come to you,' I finished. 'Where else could I go?'

'I'm glad you came,' she said quietly. 'We can do something for her. She can stop here tonight, and tomorrow we'll figure something out.'

'That's great,' I said. 'Just let her stay long enough to get in touch with her lawyer and wind up her affairs. Then she'll make a fresh start. She won't be able to go back there.'

There was a thoughtful look in Cora's eyes. 'What was the name again of the fella that got killed?' she asked.

'Arthur Kirk,' I told her.

'I used to know a fella named Kirk,' she said. Then she shrugged her shoulders and smiled. 'I guess it's a common name.'

'She's tired out,' I said, nodding at Virginia. 'What say we get her to bed? I'll drop by tomorrow and see how things are going.'

'She's sound asleep,' said Cora. 'Pity to wake her. Can you carry her in?'

Virginia didn't stir when I picked her up and carried her through to the bedroom. She gave a kinda sigh as between us we stripped off the coat and worked one of Cora's nightdresses over her head.

'Tomorrow, all this will seem like a nightmare to her,' said Cora.

'A pretty vivid nightmare.'

'She'll get over it all right,' said Cora confidently.

She bent down and examined Virginia more closely. 'She'll need soaking in a hot bath for hours,' she said, pointing. There were still particles of tar adhering to the soft underarm down.

'I did my best,' I defended. 'You couldn't expect her to be spotless.'

'A good hot bath,' she repeated. 'She'll be as good as new then.'

'And a proper haircut,' I added.

We stood looking down at Virginia. She was sleeping peacefully, her cheek nestled against the white pillow and one arm outflung. But there was a tiny pucker on her forehead, reflecting the strain of the ordeal she had undergone. Somehow she looked so childish and pathetic. I got a kinda lump in my throat. Almost paternally I bent over her and kissed her gently on the lips.

When I straightened up, Cora was looking at me with a strange, speculative look in her eyes.

'I won't keep you up any longer,' I said. 'I'll look in again tomorrow.'

She accompanied me to the door, and that same speculative look was in her eyes when she asked: 'How do you like that dame?'

I stared at her. 'She's a nice kid.'

'You kissed her.'

'I'm crazy that way. I'm often doing it.'

'It musta been embarrassing for you; cleaning her up, I

mean.'

'It was just a job. Something that had to be done.'

'But afterwards?' she said. 'Just the two of you alone …'

She left her sentence unfinished, but I knew what she meant. I chuckled. 'Nothing like that, Cora. It never crossed my mind.' Then I stopped being amused, and looked at Cora thoughtfully. 'What's biting you, anyway?' I asked. 'You getting jealous or something?'

She should have laughed, taken that as a joke. Surprisingly she didn't. Her face clouded, became almost angry, and she bundled me out of her apartment.

'To hell with you,' she said. 'You just make me mad.'

She closed the door firmly, and I heard the night-bolt being rammed home. I scratched my head, fumbled for a cigarette and shrugged my shoulders ruefully. If I hadn't known better, I'd have thought that Cora was getting jealous. But how can a dame be jealous who is forty below zero at necking time?

I fumbled my way down the darkened stairs out to the parking lot, and all the time my head was in a whirl. It's always the same where women are concerned. You just never know where you stand.

It was almost dawn when I got back to my flat. I disconnected the doorbell, wedged a sock into the telephone bell, and fell on my bed without taking off more than my shoes. I was good and tired, thoroughly exhausted and like a damp dishcloth.

I went to sleep so fast I didn't even know I'd rested my head on the pillows.

It's incredible how things work out. For Virginia, everything worked out perfectly. Hot baths, a good hairdresser, a good dressmaker and two or three days' rest produced a Virginia better than new.

And everything fitted in. It transpired that Virginia had a voice. Furthermore, she had personality and Southern charm. Cora was able to employ Virginia as a hostess.

A hostess in the Two Spot was a good job. Cora didn't employ floozies to vamp the male customers to upstairs bedrooms. The Two Spot wasn't that kinda joint. Virginia's job was to sing an occasional number and be a dancing partner, if the partner was really interested in dancing.

I guess it wasn't the kinda work that Virginia was cut out to do. But it was a job and it kept her going. It gave her a respite while she employed Chicago lawyers to negotiate for the sale and transfer of her property to the city.

And to clinch everything, the apartment next to Cora's became vacant. Virginia moved out from Cora's and took over the one next door.

It looked like, after having a tough time, things were really breaking the right way for Virginia.

I got plenty of kudos writing up the story of the tarring and feathering. But I didn't write it up fully. I left out the essential details of where Virginia had escaped to and my part in her escape.

I dropped in a couple times at the Two Spot to see Virginia, and she was doing okay. And then, on account of a news angle I was following, I kept outta the Two Spot for five whole days in a row. The sixth day, I got a telephone call from Virginia.

'I've got to see you, Hank. It's important. Terribly important.'

I could sense the fear in her voice.

'Don't upset yourself, honey. Sure you can see me. I'll come right away.'

'I don't want you to do that, Hank,' she said. 'But will you see me tonight at the Two Spot? Come at half-past seven. Don't be later. It's terribly important.'

'Sure,' I said. 'But tell me what it is about.'

'I can't, Hank,' she said. 'Not now. Do please wait until tonight.'

'Okay,' I said. 'I'll be there.'

I got to the Two Spot dead on time. I had time to join Ben Hilton in a drink at the bar before Virginia whisked me away. Ben, swaying almost imperceptibly, winked owlishly as she took me by the arm.

'What's worrying you?' I demanded.

'Don't talk yet,' she said. 'Come with me.'

She led me off to a small room that was usually reserved for private parties, and carefully closed the door.

'Well?' I demanded. 'Why so secretive?'

She was agitated. Her fingers kept clasping and unclasping nervously. There was a flush on her cheeks and an excited sparkle to her green eyes. I looked her over slowly. The hairdresser had worked wonders. She had the urchin cut, which gave her a cheeky look, and her arms and shoulders were bare. The pale blue evening gown she was wearing was backless and strapless.

'I'm in trouble, Hank,' she said simply.

It was the first time we'd been alone together since the day we'd first met. Seeing her bare neck and shoulders shimmering beneath the light reminded me suddenly and urgently of the way she'd looked on the river bank, lying on her belly, chin in hand and the soft curve of her breasts exposed, fascinating and exciting.

'Sure, you're in trouble,' I said thickly, and moved in. I slid my arm around her waist and my other arm around her shoulder. My fingers tingled as they contacted her smooth skin, and her lips were warm and moist, becoming at once hot and urgent.

And then she was pushing me away. 'We haven't much time, Hank,' she pleaded. She was breathing heavily and her lipstick was smudged. The bodice of her gown had become disarranged. One side had slipped down.

'What's so damned important it can't wait,' I demanded. I was breathing heavily myself. She put her hands gently against my chest as I reached for her again.

'Please, Hank, not now,' she protested. 'I'm in trouble. You've got to help.'

'All right,' I growled thickly and reluctantly. I scowled and fumbled for a cigarette, giving my hands something else to do. She gave her bodice a tug so that the tip of her breast slipped back into mysterious obscurity.

'It's Lew Kirk,' she said 'He's here. In Chicago.'

I stopped with the match half-way to my cigarette. 'Lew Kirk!'

She nodded. 'He's traced me here,' she said. 'He telephoned today. Insisted I should see him.'

I got myself under control. I struck another match and blew smoke through my nostrils. I did that to give myself time to think.

'How did he trace you?'

'I suppose it was easy,' she confessed. 'Now that Arthur Kirk is dead, Lew Kirk has taken over his business. That means that Lew Kirk is my guardian. The lawyers I employed had to get in touch with him about my estate. I imagine he got my address from them.'

'Yeah. I guess so.' I puffed some more smoke. 'Are you going to see him?'

She nodded. 'He'll be here any minute. But I wanted you to be here with me. I feel safe when you're around.'

'You act like you're scared.'

'It's probably Kirk,' she said. 'I told Ben and Cora about it. They said I could interview him in this room.'

Right then there was a knock at the door. I raised my voice. 'Who's there?' I yelled.

Ben Hilton said through the panels: 'There's a coupla guys here asking to see Virginia.'

I looked at her steadily. She clenched her hands tightly and then nodded her head.

'Let 'em in, Ben,' I called. 'Let them in.'

Lew Kirk may have been surprised to see me. But if he was, he didn't show it. There was a greasy grin of satisfaction on his face as he nodded genially at me and Virginia. 'Allow me to present my friend, Mr Duff,' he said blandly.

Mr Duff was a shrivelled-up little guy with a withered face and two very big buck teeth. He nodded at me and Virginia, and his little ferret eyes flicked from one to the other of us as though he daren't look at either of us for more than a second at a time.

Ben Hilton carefully closed the door behind them, and Lew Kirk chuckled, pulled out a chair for himself and settled down comfortably. Duff stood behind him, his arm resting on the back of the chair and his eyes still flicking like he used them for semaphore signals.

'You're looking well, Virginia,' said Kirk smugly.

I put myself between him and Virginia. I clenched my right fist into a ball and massaged it with my left hand. I lowered my head slightly and said softly, 'I wouldn't bother Virginia, if I were you.'

His face reflected mock surprise. 'I don't want to bother Virginia,' he said. 'I want to stop her from making a fool of herself.'

'Meaning what?'

He grinned and waved his cigarette airily. 'I don't have to tell you. You're a sensible guy. You know the kinda jam Virginia got into.' He arched his neck to see around me. 'She came out of it all right, it seems.'

'So what?' I gritted.

He shrugged his shoulders. 'That's all over, now,' he said. 'Naturally, Virginia can't go back. But she can start a new life. She's got plenty of dough. The past is dead. She can make a new life for herself.'

'Come to the point,' I said. 'Cut the fancy talk.'

'Well, you know how it is. Publicity's a terrible thing. Stories! The papers would just be dying for a story about a dame who got tarred and feathered. I guess if they knew she was around Chicago they just wouldn't leave her alone. I guess everywhere she went she would be known as the dame who was tarred and feathered.'

I moved in just a little closer, lowered my head just a little more, and clenched my left fist as well as my right. 'Just say it,' I said. 'Go on, say it.'

He looked at me uneasily, smirked weakly and said: 'I wouldn't like to know Virginia had the finger put on her. She's here in Chicago. Nobody knows a thing about her. It'd be much better that way, wouldn't it?'

'It had better stop that way, too,' I said ominously.

'I'm glad we see eye to eye.' He flicked the ash from his cigarette, and watched it fall to the ground. Then he said slowly, 'Cooperation always achieves the best results. Naturally I'm only too anxious to cooperate with Virginia. In return, she should cooperate with me.' He watched me warily, and said: 'I'm a little short of dough at the moment.'

I'd been waiting for it. I swayed back on my heels and drew back my left fist. But that was all I did. The little wizened guy had moved quickly. His eyes were flicking no more. They were levelled straight at me with ferret-like intensity. And he was holding in his hand just about the longest, keenest, ugliest-looking knife I'd ever seen; and the way he held it warned me he was a past-master at the art of slipping in under a swinging fist and sliding that knife home as neatly and as cleanly as a bullfighter slides his sword into the heart of a bull.

'I wouldn't like you to fall on that while we're having a little business talk,' said Lew blandly.

I swallowed hard. 'You ain't always going to have that knife merchant around,' I pointed out.

Lew shrugged his shoulders. 'Don't let's be sidetracked. The issue is simple. Shall the newspapers know Virginia is the dame who was tarred and feathered, or is she willing to make over to me half of her estate?'

I breathed heavily. 'You can't get away with blackmail.'

'But I can,' he purred. 'I assure you I can.' He fumbled in his inside pocket and pulled out a legal-looking document. 'You see, I have everything prepared. This document entitles me to one half of Virginia's estate. This is a gift in consideration of the services of my brother and myself while we were her guardians. You will notice there are two other places for witnesses to sign. Mr Duff will be one witness, and I suggest you are the other witness.'

'You're crazy,' I said. 'Virginia won't sign anything like that.'

He shrugged his shoulders. 'I hoped that she would,' he said. 'I could do with some financial assistance right now.' He shrugged his shoulders again. 'Otherwise, I'm afraid Mr Duff and I will have to spend some money telephoning the newspapers.'

'Get out,' I said.

Kirk looked at his watch. 'I'll give Virginia five minutes to decide,' he said. 'The nature of this interview is such that it must be settled now or not at all. You have five minutes, Virginia, my dear. You sign or else you take the consequences.'

I was trembling with anger. 'Get out,' I mouthed. I made half a step forward, and Duff made a corresponding menacing gesture with that long knife. It was an efficient gesture, so rapid I almost felt the cold steel cutting into my belly and stirring my entrails.

At the same moment I felt Virginia's fingers on my arm.

'We can't let him do it, Hank. I couldn't face it. Not all that. I'd die. I'd kill myself or something.'

'You can't give in to him,' I said hotly. 'That would be just the beginning. He'd bleed you white.'

The door of the room wasn't locked. It burst open quite suddenly. Kirk spun around to face the door. But Duff wasn't to be put off. He still stood staring at me with that long knife pointing hungrily toward my belly.

Ben Hilton was framed in the doorway, swaying imperceptibly, his eyes sparkling a little too brightly and his cheeks flushed. Behind him were two burly figures. One was Jake, who stoked the furnace, and the other was Colin, Cora's chauffeur.

Kirk demanded: 'What the hell do you want?'

Ben said quietly: 'Okay, boys. Take him.'

Jake and Colin circled the room toward Kirk in a businesslike manner. Ben carefully closed the door, locked it and leaned with his back against it. Kirk's face was a shade paler when he said quickly, 'Duff!'

Duff's eyes began flicking again. They flicked from me to Colin, and from Colin to Jake. That was a lotta work for one pair of eyes to do. Especially when Jake and Colin were moving in from the rear.

Duff suddenly realised he wasn't in a healthy position. He promptly abandoned Kirk and ran to the wall, where he stood with his back protected. His upper lip was raised, exposing his two buck teeth, and he made a low snarling noise. The long knife gleamed ominously in his hand.

Jake dealt with Kirk smoothly and efficiently. He grabbed him by the collar and half lifted him out of his chair before slamming his first hard against his jaw. Kirk slammed back against the chair so hard it toppled backwards. Kirk lay where he had fallen, moaning softly and painfully, spitting out bits of broken teeth.

Duff was the dangerous character. We left Kirk lying where he was and stood around Duff in a semicircle. He snarled at us like a rat at bay. He made quick, angry movements with that long knife, that sent cold shudders down my spine.

It looked like it was going to be stalemate until Colin picked up a chair, levelled it horizontally and then suddenly ran straight at Duff. Duff tried to avoid it and then tried to fight it. There was a flash as the long knife flickered through the air, and then a savage scream of pain as one chair-leg buried itself in Duff's belly and another gouged his scrawny neck. The knife clattered to the floor, and I dived for it and kicked it across the room.

Without the knife, Duff was finished. Jake cuffed him leisurely, and Duff fell on the ground beside Kirk, where he lay, apprehensively flicking his eyes from one to the other of us.

'Get 'em up,' said Ben. I looked at him quickly. He seemed to know exactly what he was doing.

'You came in at just the right time,' I said.

He nodded, but didn't seem to notice me. 'Sit 'em up,' he said. Then, when Kirk and Duff were seated, Ben jerked his head at Colin. 'Get the evidence,' he said.

Kirk sat there mopping at his bleeding lips with his handkerchief. He shot venomous glances at all of us, and especially at Duff. Ben sat on the edge of the table and drew a flask from his pocket. He took a sip, wiped his lips, sighed with satisfaction, and put the flask back in his hip pocket. Then he looked at Kirk and said slowly: 'You've cooked yourself, fella.'

Kirk's eyes flicked from Ben's to Virginia's. 'She's cooked herself, too,' he said. There was a look of bitter hatred in his eyes.

Ben shook his head slowly. 'You haven't heard it all yet, fella,' he said. 'Just you wait.'

Colin came back just then. He was carrying a kinda portable gramophone. Ben got up off the table and the gramophone was set down and plugged into a power-socket. It wasn't until then that I had an inkling of what was happening.

When Ben switched on and the room began to fill with the recorded voices of myself, Kirk and Virginia, Kirk's face turned white.

It was all there. All of it. A complete record of an attempt at blackmail. When the recording was finished, Ben Hilton tilted up the table to show the concealed microphone.

'Okay, Colin, take it away and keep it safe,' said Ben.

Kirk licked his lips nervously. The wizened Duff seemed to shrink even more into his chair. Ben said slowly:

'Blackmail's a mighty serious offence. I don't have to tell you.'

Kirk blustered. 'It's a frame-up. I wasn't trying to blackmail anybody.'

Ben leaned forward and tapped his finger on the table. 'It's this way, Kirk. You're gonna keep your trap shut. And any time the papers make even the slightest mention about Virginia and tar and feathers, that evidence is going straight to the cops. Do I make myself clear?'

Kirk dropped his eyes and said nothing.

Ben leaned forward and slapped his face hard. 'Do I make myself clear?' he demanded.

Kirk nodded weakly.

Ben seemed satisfied. 'That goes for both of you,' he said. 'You're both blackmailers. And if you make just one squawk, the cops get that recording.'

Colin came back. He nodded as he met Ben's enquiring eyes. 'Locked away safe,' he said cheerfully.

'Okay,' said Ben. Then he jerked his head toward Duff and Kirk. 'Just work on those two boys a little. Teach them a lesson.'

Jake and Colin were big guys. They knew how to punch and how to make a punch hurt. It wasn't a very big room, and a lotta furniture got smashed up. Virginia couldn't bear to see it. She buried her face against my chest. I liked that. When I put my arms around her protectively, my fingers tingled from the contact of her soft skin. Ben Hilton stood there, swaying imperceptibly, from time to time taking out the brandy flask and treating himself to a nip.

Colin and Jake were efficient. They took very little time. When they were through, Duff and Kirk looked very, very sorry for themselves. Their eyes were blackened, their faces were bleeding, and beneath their clothes they musta been black and blue all over.

'All right,' said Ben casually. 'Now throw them out.'

They carried Duff out first. When they got back for Kirk he was still lying on the floor, whimpering with pain. He flinched away from them as they grabbed his arms and pulled him to his feet. He was slobbering as they dragged him to the doorway, knees buckling beneath him.

Ben opened the door just as Cora was entering. She barely glanced at Kirk as she asked: 'You handled everything, Ben?'

'Perfectly, Cora,' he grinned. He swayed back on his heels and drew hard on his cigarette.

'Get this one outside, quick,' said Cora curtly. 'Don't let anybody see him.'

I was watching her at the time. I saw her gaze slip casually toward Kirk and then slip away again. And then her eyes flicked back quickly, showing recognition. Her eyes widened and there was a gleam of horror deep down behind them. She gave a kinda gasp.

Ben noticed it, too. 'What's the matter, Cora?'

'Nothing,' she said quickly. 'Nothing.' But her face had gone white. And Kirk! His glazed eyes had glanced up at her. He opened his lips and mumbled something brokenly.

'Get him out of here quick,' said Cora, and then, as Colin

and Jake dragged him away, she followed them with her eyes.

'What's the matter, Cora?' asked Ben, gently.

She spun round on him angrily, her eyes blazing. 'Who is that man?' she demanded.

'Kirk,' I said. 'Lew Kirk.'

Cora's eyes turned to me, and suddenly they seemed wild. She was beyond herself. She paced across to me and demanded loudly: 'Why did you let him come here? Why did you let him come?'

Virginia said, surprised: 'But you knew about it, Cora. I told you. You and Ben arranged about the microphone ...'

For a moment red anger flared high in Cora's eyes, and it seemed she would strike Virginia. For a moment she battled to get control of herself. Then she spun on her heel and walked toward the door.

Ben said: 'Cora, my dear. If there's anything the matter ...'

'Get the hell out of it,' she snapped, and pushed him savagely away.

She slammed the door so hard it almost broke from its hinges. Me and Virginia stared at Ben. He stared back, and then with an eloquent gesture that almost equalled the French, he spread his hands and shrugged his shoulders.

'What a dame,' he said. 'What a dame.'

10

The next morning I got a call from the Superintendent of the morgue attached to the Missing Person's Bureau.

'Busy, Hank?'

'What's on your mind?'

'Busy time last night. Picked up a bunch of stiffs. Like to come over and take a look?'

Any corpse is liable to be news. 'Sure,' I said. 'I'll be right over.'

I dropped the story I was working on and went straight over. The white-coated attendant knew me well enough. He nodded his head in greeting and said: 'Guess you heard we had a busy time?'

'Gang fight?'

'No,' he said thoughtfully. He finished chewing the matchstick in the corner of his mouth and spat it out on the floor. 'Just a busy night. Coming?'

I followed him through the corridors and down the stone steps to the basement where they kept them on ice until they were shovelled into the furnace. It was cold, dreary and eerie down in that basement. We walked along another stone corridor, with our footsteps echoing strangely. We stopped opposite a thick wooden door and he slid back long bolts.

I never did learn why they have bolts on those doors. I've seen plenty of occupants of the morgue and none of them looked to me like they were going places.

He pushed open the door, reached inside and switched on the lights as I followed him in. It was cooler still inside. A little shiver ran down my spine. But it wasn't only the cold that caused it. I always get that kinda feeling when I visit these places.

He chuckled grimly, rubbed his hands with satisfaction and said loudly, 'Quite a bag, huh? Four of 'em.'

There were four of them right enough. Four cold, still mounds beneath white shrouds. The slabs they were lying on were white marble. It suddenly seemed much colder in there, and I became acutely conscious of the pungent odour of antiseptic.

It was all in the day's work to the morgue assistant. He talked cheerfully as he led the way to the first slab.

He pulled back the sheet, stripping it right down. There was a middle-aged guy lying there, looking strangely waxen.

His naked body wore cuts and abrasions from knee to shoulder.

'This guy was knocked down by a hit-and-run driver. Wore good clothes. A guy with plenty of dough, I should say. Somebody's pretty certain to claim him before long.'

I nodded, taking in the ugly headwound that had killed him. Even now that it had been cleaned up and made to look pretty, it made my belly queasy.

He pulled the sheet up over the still face and moved to the next slab. 'This one's quite a dish,' he said. 'Found her floating in the lake. Couldn't have been in more than a coupla hours.'

He pulled down the sheet to show me the still figure of a blonde, about 25. She'd been a good-looking dame. She musta died by drowning, because her body was that bluish colour that comes as a result of asphyxiation. And there was an ugly blue lump on her forehead.

'Too nice a dame to finish that way,' I said.

He shrugged. 'It happens to all kinda folks.'

'How did she get the bump?' I asked. 'Before or after she hit the water?'

'That's what Homicide are working on,' he said. 'She got

socked and thrown in.' He beckoned me closer. 'Take a look at this, fella.'

He got hold of her and rolled her over. It was all in the day's work to him. But I hated it. She was stiff as a board and as cold as ice. Her unnatural stiffness as he levered her onto her side got those queasy feelings deep down in my belly working overtime.

'Take a look at this.'

I went around his side and looked at the small of the dame's back. There were four blue, rigid wheals that coulda been caused by a viciously wielded strap.

'And what d'ya make of this?' he demanded.

His forefinger indicated an indented impression completely encircling the dame's waist. I hadn't noticed it at first, due to the bluish tinge of her skin. But when I looked close I could see it was the kinda impression a fine chain might have made if drawn tightly around her waist and kept that way for several days.

'Looks like it was caused by a chain,' I said.

He nodded. 'That's what the cops think.' He let her drop back onto the slab, and her shoulders hitting the marble made a noise like frozen meat hitting a butcher's slab.

'I don't know how you can handle them every day like you do.'

He shrugged. 'Just a job, brother. Just a job.' He shook his head sadly. 'Quite a dish, ain't she?' Then he clucked his tongue. 'Just think, fella. A coupla days ago, this dame dressed the way she is now would have got me champing at the bit.'

He shrugged his shoulders again and began to draw the white shroud over her. 'And right now,' he concluded thoughtfully, 'I can spend all the time I want looking at her curves and it don't mean a thing.'

'Maybe it's just as well,' I said drily. 'Otherwise someday you'd be running off to the Registrar trying to get hitched to one of your customers.'

He chuckled as he led the way to the next slab. 'Now, this guy,' he said. He screwed up his brow, trying to remember.

Then he pulled away the white shroud and consulted the tag tied to the big toe. That refreshed his memory.

'Oh yeah,' he said. 'This is an old guy.'

I could tell it was an old guy. He looked about a hundred and fifty. Maybe a hundred and sixty.

'Night cop found him on a park seat. Musta died that way. Just an old tramp. No letters, no money, no anything except fleas. And even the fleas passed him up when he got cold.'

'Maybe this is the first peace he's ever known,' I said. 'There ain't nothing for me there.'

We drifted along to the fourth slab. 'This is a Homicide case without a doubt,' said the morgue assistant. 'Night cop found him in an alley. Got a knife through his ribs. Musta been a long knife. It came out the other side.'

He whisked off the sheet and I stood staring down at the guy stretched out, clean and washed. Just beneath the ribs, the even line of a narrow wound showed where the knife had entered.

I stood looking down at him, clenching my hands tightly so that my nails dug into the palms, and tried to keep my face under control. I said in a voice that seemed strange in my own ears, 'How far did the cops get?'

'You'd better ask up at Homicide,' he said. 'Those fellas are pretty clammy. All I know is, they found him in an alley. No identification.'

My mouth was dry and I wanted a drink. 'The cops didn't talk like they knew who to hang it on?'

He leered. 'They keep their traps shut. That's what they do when they can't make the grade. Chances are, if he ain't identified they'll slide him to the crematorium pretty smart. Homicide's pretty busy these days. They got all the work they want.' He nodded at the man on the slab. 'He don't look the kinda guy folks would fall in love with, does he?'

'Thanks for the show,' I said.

He draped the sheet over the fourth figure and I peeled a fin off my wad. He pocketed it smoothly and winked. 'Any time you like, Hank,' he said. 'Any time.'

I got outside quickly and crossed the road to a bar. I had two double whiskies in quick succession, and the thoughts kept whirling around in my head like bluebottles around a meat-cover.

I didn't want to think it. But everything added up one way. And the more I thought about it and the more obvious it became, the angrier I grew.

I paid for my drinks and flagged a taxi right outside the bar. And all the way to Cora's apartment I was thinking about it and seeing it even more clearly and getting madder and madder.

I went up the stairs to Cora's apartment three at a time. I kept my thumb on the bell-push until a trimly-dressed maid opened the door. I brushed past her roughly into the entrance hall.

The maid, a little dark-haired dame with bright eyes like buttons and a starched cap and apron, did her best. 'You really can't push in here like this,' she protested.

'Is Cora in?' I demanded.

'If you wish to see Miss Reid and give me your name ...'

'Is Cora in?' I roared.

She looked frightened. She swallowed nervously and said, 'Miss Reid is in, but I'll have to tell her you're ...'

I didn't wait. I was walking along the corridor into the living-room with the maid chasing along behind me. Cora wasn't in the living-room. I barged straight across the living-room toward the bedroom door. The maid came after me, protesting tearfully, 'You can't go in there, sir. I'll have to tell Miss Reid that you're here ...'

I thrust open the door of the bedroom. The coverlets were pulled down but the room was empty. There was another door opening off the bedroom, which led to Cora's large and expensive bathroom. The bathroom door was half open and I heard voices.

The maid made one more frantic attempt to stop me as I strode across the bedroom toward the bathroom door. She clutched me by the arm. I shook her off angrily, and then she stood and watched me with wide eyes, one hand clapped over her mouth.

I put my shoulder against the bathroom door and barged in. It was a big bathroom. It had everything. All in marble and chromium fittings. It was the kinda bathroom Cleopatra or Caesar would have been jealous about.

Cora was there. She was lying outstretched on a massage table. One end of the table was raised so she was kinda sitting up. There was a dame with her. A white-coated dame who had her sleeves rolled up to her elbows and both hands covered in what looked like tar. It was this dame that gave the shrill cry of alarm. As for Cora, my bursting in that way caused her no sign of surprise other than a faint raising of the eyebrows.

'I want you, Cora,' I said, breathing hard. I guess I must have looked pretty angry.

The white-aproned dame squealed at me. 'How dare you! You can't come in here. How dare you!'

What worried the white-coated dame was the fact that Cora was stark naked. She was getting some kinda beauty treatment. That black stuff was a kinda face pack for the body. The white-coated dame was busy smearing it on Cora. So far she had covered Cora's neck and shoulders. That left a whole lot more to do, and a whole lot of Cora that was uncovered.

'Get out, get out,' screamed the white-coated dame. 'You can't come in here. Get out!'

'I want you, Cora,' I said at the same time. 'You and me have got to talk.'

The white-coated dame picked up a hand-towel about the size of a postage stamp and frantically began trying to cover Cora with it. In her flurry, she jabbed her elbow against Cora's mouth. It was a painful jab. Cora snatched at the towel and hurled it across the room.

'Get out, will you, and stop that damned screaming,' she yelled at the woman.

The woman gaped. She looked from my angry face to Cora's white, set face, and then back to me again.

'For heaven's sake get out when you are told,' snapped Cora irritably.

The woman gave Cora one more startled look and then scurried out through the door. She glanced over her shoulder and pointedly left the bathroom door open.

I crossed to the bathroom door and closed it. I turned the key in the lock. I guessed the masseuse and the maid would have a lot to talk about. But that was as nothing compared with what I had to talk to Cora about.

She was sitting there now, apparently unmoved, her eyes probing into me and only her raised eyebrows showing her annoyance.

'Now what the hell do you mean by this?' she demanded imperiously.

'I've stood for a lot, Cora,' I said. 'But this time you've gone too far. I'm going out. I'm washing my hands of everything.'

'What the devil are you talking about?'

'Do I have to draw a picture?' I sneered. 'There were two guys here last night. Lew Kirk and a little guy named Duff. You knew they were coming, which was more than I did.'

'And what if I did?'

'What you did last night, I agreed with,' I said. 'Kirk was a blackmailer. Blackmailers don't deserve to get consideration. You and Ben handled them just right.'

'Well, what's eating you?'

'Beating a coupla guys up is one thing,' I said. 'Murder's another.'

There was dead silence in the room. The silence seemed to go on for hours and hours. Cora's expression didn't change. Her eyes still probed into me. Finally she said quietly, 'Murder?'

'Yeah. And I want nothing to do with it. I'm telling you now, Cora, I'm going right outta here. I owe it to you to keep my mouth closed. I'm not going to the cops. But if the cops come for me, I've got to tell them what I know.'

Strangely, crazily, a look of hopefulness came into her eyes. 'Murder, Hank?' she whispered. 'Who was killed? Tell me, quick.'

I narrowed my eyes. 'A little guy,' I said. 'The little guy Duff. Looks like he was stabbed with his own knife.'

The crazy, happy look in her eyes evaporated. Her eyes became cool and indifferent and probing. 'The little man Duff was killed?'

I nodded.

'And you think I did it?'

'Don't let's be childish about it,' I said angrily. 'Maybe you didn't actually do it. But it happened by your instructions.'

She said quietly: 'My boys didn't kill Duff.'

I looked at her keenly. 'You ain't trying to lead me by the nose?'

'Don't take my word for it,' she said. 'My boys took them right outside and dropped them in the gutter. The beat cop saw it all. It cost ten bucks to buy his silence. You can check with that cop anytime you like. Kirk and his pal were picked up right away by the taxi. That's the last we saw of them.'

The anger simmering inside me was lukewarm now. 'Gee, Cora, what else was I to think?' I blustered.

'Think what you like,' she snapped. 'Any time a guy gets bumped off, just come running around and accuse me. I just love it.'

I became suddenly conscious of what a fool I'd been. 'I'm real sorry,' I said. 'I guess I wasn't thinking.'

She was sitting there, quietly, her face calm and serene. But a little smile was tugging at the corner of her lips. 'Okay, you're sorry,' she said. 'But you don't have to stand on one leg, shamefaced, looking like a naughty schoolboy.'

'I guess I oughta known better,' I said. 'But seeing him stretched out there in the morgue gave me a kinda shock. I just started adding up two and two, and made five.'

While I was speaking, I idly picked up the pot of black stuff. The instructions read: *To keep your skin smooth and fresh, lightly apply a thin coating of Pretar, allow to dry for half-an-hour and then wash off with hot soapy water.*

'You want some feathers to go with this?'

Her eyes laughed and her cheeks dimpled. 'Every woman likes to be beautiful,' she said.

I dipped two fingers into the jar, scooped up a chunk of the mixture and held it beneath my nostrils. It smelled very faintly of decaying vegetation. 'What's it matter if you're beautiful or not? When you get a guy interested, there ain't anything you wanna do.'

'Perhaps,' she said softly, 'I admire beauty for its own sake.'

'That's what fellas have to do where you're concerned,' I pointed out. I looked around for somewhere to wipe the stuff off my fingers. The logical place seemed to be on Cora. I wiped it off onto her skin and gently spread it along her calf. As my fingers touched her, I sensed her tense. Then she relaxed.

'Sorry I made you chase out the masseuse.'

She didn't answer. I glanced up at her and she dropped her eyelids. Beneath them she was watching my hand smearing Pretar over her white skin.

'You're not too bad at it yourself,' she said.

'I'm wizard at it,' I grinned. I scooped out a handful of the messy stuff, slapped it on her leg and smeared it down toward her ankle, coating her dainty foot and in between her toes.

She twiddled her toes. 'Hey,' she said. 'That tickles.'

'There was a nasty case down in the morgue this morning,' I said, conversationally. I was in the mood for talking. 'A nice-looking dame got fished out the water.'

'Accident?'

I frowned. 'Got a bump on her head. Coulda been an accident. Coulda been murder.' I slapped another dollop of Pretar on Cora's thigh, and smeared it around. I wasn't thinking what I was doing. I was thinking of how that dame in the morgue had looked.

'Looked like somebody had been giving her the work-over,' I said. 'Marks on her back where she'd been beaten.'

'Really,' said Cora politely.

I smeared the stuff over Cora's legs. Her knees were pressed tightly together, but they parted naturally beneath the pressure of my fingers. I continued smearing Pretar along the inside of her thigh.

'There was a kinda mark around her waist,' I went on. 'The kinda mark a chain would have made if it had been pulled tight and kept that way for several days.'

She made a funny kinda noise.

'All kinda things happen in a big town,' I went on, still thinking about the blonde and still absentmindedly smearing Pretar.

Cora moved her legs. Just slightly. But enough for me to notice her limbs had taken on a strange rigidity. I glanced up at her and stared.

There was a wild, strange look in Cora's eyes as she stared back at me. And she thrust her forearm into her mouth like she was trying to bite it.

'Feeling hungry?' I asked.

She just stared at me with that strange, wild light in her eyes and her teeth clamped firmly.

I got worried. 'Are you crazy or something? You'll hurt yourself that way.'

She went on staring at me and still went on biting. I saw muscles knotting at the corners of her jaws as she tried to clamp her teeth together; and then, suddenly, the blood spurted out from between her lips.

I dropped the jar I was holding and grabbed Cora's wrist. I put my other hand against her forehead and levered. I figured she must have suddenly gone crazy or something. 'Stop it,' I yelled. 'Stop it, will ya?'

I was afraid to exert too much effort. She might have bitten a chunk of her arm clean out. I kept yelling at her, tried prying her jaws apart, and all the time the blood was running in a red stream from between her lips and dripping onto her bare breasts.

I couldn't let her go on doing that, and although the alternative wasn't pleasant, I had to do it. I socked her hard on the side of the jaw. She gave a kinda sigh and relaxed. Even then I had a job prying her jaws apart.

She'd bitten into the fleshy part of her arm. Her teeth had sunk deep and her arm was bleeding profusely. But it wasn't serious. I cleaned it up, stopped the bleeding and was covering it with sticking plaster by the time she came around.

She glanced at her arm, and then her eyes switched to mine. There was a strange expression in her eyes, but they weren't wild any longer.

'How d'ya feel?' I asked.

She touched the side of her jaw tenderly. 'Not too bad,' she said. 'Will you get me a drink?'

'Sure.' I unlocked the bathroom door, went through the bedroom and into the living-room. The maid and the masseuse were standing there, chattering excitedly. They froze into silence when I appeared. I ignored them, grabbed a bottle of whisky and a glass from the sideboard and went back to the bathroom.

I guess Cora would have looked strange to anyone else, the way she was, with her neck and shoulders covered in Pretar and one leg smeared with it as far as her hips. But it didn't seem very funny to me right then. I was worried about her. I splashed whisky into the glass until it reached the brim. I gave it to her that way, neat, and she drained it in one gulp.

'That good?' I asked.

She nodded, and once again tenderly touched her jaw. 'You pack a wallop,' she commented.

'I'm sorry about that.'

Her eyes were watching me, eyes that were strange. 'I guess you had to do it,' she said.

'Yeah. What happened? You went crazy or something. Looked like you were gonna gnaw your arm off.'

She gave an exasperated kinda sigh. 'You would ask what happened. Can't you guess?'

'Maybe you've had a lotta strain recently,' I said sympathetically. 'What say you take a holiday?'

Another exasperated sigh. And then suddenly, angrily, 'You caused it, you dumb dope. You made me do it.'

'Me!' I looked at her incredulously.

'Do you find that so surprising?' she said, wearily. 'Can't you imagine why?'

I looked sheepish. 'Well, I guess it was kinda upsetting, me rushing in here like that and accusing you of murdering Duff.'

She laughed. A hard, brittle laugh. It sounded false and she broke it off abruptly when she saw me eyeing her anxiously.

'Hadn't it occurred to you,' she said, with a sarcastic inflexion in her voice, 'that it might have been caused by you touching me?'

I understood then: I'd been smearing her with Pretar. And it got me angry. Every guy's got a streak of vanity, and no guy likes to have his vanity knocked cold.

'All right,' I rasped bitterly. 'I'll keep away from you. I'll keep good and away. I won't come within a mile of you. If you find my touch is so detestable that you wanna chew yourself to pieces, I won't cause you grief by letting you see me at all.'

I was angry. But that was nothing compared with the way she got angry. She sat upright, and her eyes still wore that strange expression, but there were angry flashes in them, too.

'Get out,' she said fiercely. 'Get out.'

'Sure, I'll get out. I can't get out quick enough.'

'Get out.' She almost spat the words at me, but her voice had sunk to a whisper.

I walked over to the bathroom door. When I got there, I turned around and gave her a contemptuous glare.

She said again. 'Get out,' but her voice had lost all of its venom. Then she added, almost in a moan: 'You fool, Hank. You damn fool.'

I closed the door behind me, stalked through the bedroom and through the living-room.

The maid and the masseuse sank into wide-eyed silence as I passed through the living-room. There must have been two red spots burning high up on my cheekbones. I felt like a whipped cur. I was humiliated and my ego was as flat as a pancake.

I slammed the door of the apartment behind me and slunk out to my car. I climbed into it feeling knee-high to a cockroach. I was wondering just how many other dames might find my touch sickening and nauseating.

And that got me good and worried. Because dames are such curious animals, you never know where you are with them.

11

Fortunately for my peace of mind I was good and busy for the next few days. I hadn't got time to ponder on my personal shortcomings. I was in up to my neck on the blonde-in-the-morgue case. Homicide picked up a few clues and I got in on in. It was quite a case, and I got quite a scoop for the paper. But all that's another story, which maybe I'll find time to write about someday.

I hadn't forgotten the incident with Cora, but I shoved it right to the back of my mind. It was better that way. It was the kinda thing it was better not to remember. But it all came back with a rush when I went into a bar and ordered a whisky and found myself elbow-to-elbow with Ben Hilton.

Ever since I'd known him he'd always been just the right side of the borderline between tipsiness and drunkenness. That day, he'd passed the borderline.

'Taking your custom elsewhere?' I asked. As manager of the Two Spot, drinks would have been on the house for him. At the same time, my mind conjured up a vision of Cora's wild, strange expression as her teeth bit deeply into her flesh.

He stared at me with troubled eyes. 'You mean the Two Spot?'

'Uh-huh.'

He shook his head sadly. 'I'm out of there, brother. I've been sacked.' He laughed bitterly. 'Me! I've been sacked.'

'What!'

'Ain't easy to believe, is it?' He tossed his drink down his throat and called for another. He was too far gone to think of ordering for me as well.

'You and Cora had trouble?'

'Me and Cora have trouble?' His eyes grew soft. 'I'd do anything for Cora. Anything!' When folks have drunk too much they tend to let down their guard. Ben Hilton let down his guard. He went on talking about Cora, about how beautiful she was and how much he loved her. It was almost as if the poor guy had bottled up all his emotions for years and this was the first time he had let them loose. They came out in a hot, passionate flood, and Ben was talking loudly. Lots of other customers became interested and listened with stupid grins on their faces.

'Okay, Ben,' I said gruffly, shutting him up. 'So Cora's a good kid. So what. So she gave you the sack.'

'Yeah,' he said moodily. 'I got the push.'

'For what?'

His blue eyes studied me carefully, if blearily, and an artful expression came into them. 'You're a clever guy,' he said. 'Maybe you can figure out the answer. What say you step along and see what goes on at the Two Spot?'

'What are you getting at?'

'That's a good idea,' he said enthusiastically. 'You go along to the Two Spot. See for yourself.'

'You can tell me just as well.'

'Oh no,' he said. 'You've got to see it for yourself before you believe it. I couldn't tell it the way it is.'

He clammed up then. I couldn't get a word out of him. Not beyond his request that I was to go to the Two Spot myself.

I left him three whiskies later, by which time he'd had probably a dozen. There wasn't much point in staying. Ben was fast asleep, sprawled over one of the tables.

I went outside into the midday sunlight and tried to decide whether I'd go back to the office or look in at the police courts. On an impulse I didn't know was there until it was working, I flagged a taxi. When the cabby asked 'Where to?' the words seemed to jump out without my thinking.

'The Two Spot nightclub.'

It was closed, of course. But I went up to Cora's apartment and she opened the door herself. She didn't seem surprised to see me, and I followed her into the living-room.

'Drink?' she asked.

I nodded. Then I watched her as she poured. A change seemed to have come over her. She seemed dull and listless. There were dull black rings around her eyes, indicating sleepless nights. She put my drink on an occasional table and slumped tiredly into a chair. She rested one hand against her forehead as though she had a headache.

'I just met Ben,' I said.

Her eyes were dull and listless. 'He told you he doesn't work here any longer?'

'That's right,' I said. 'Doesn't seem to know why he got the sack.'

'I didn't give him any reason.'

'Want to talk about it?'

'Why don't you mind your own business,' she said wearily.

I got up slowly. I said grimly: 'Ben Hilton stood by you a long time. He didn't quit when the going was poor. He stuck. It's a lousy business to throw him out now.'

'All right, Hank,' she said quietly. 'That's enough. Finish your drink and go.'

I picked up my drink. I balanced it in my hand, and then slowly and deliberately I flung it across the room. The glass smashed against the wall and liquor spattered the furniture. Cora's dull eyes watched uninterestedly. 'Will you go now?' she asked.

'Sure,' I said. 'I'll go.'

I was half-way across the room when I heard the key in the door of her apartment. I turned and looked enquiringly at Cora, and she'd gone white. There was a wild, hunted expression in her eyes.

When Lew Kirk strode down the passageway and into the living-room it took the wind right out of my sails. I gaped at him. But he had himself under control. He glanced at me, his eyes flicked to Cora and grinned mockingly, and then his eyes flicked back to me. 'Don't go on my account,' he said.

I got my breath back. I turned to Cora. 'What's this lug doing here?'

She didn't even look at me. She was looking at Kirk. There was apprehension in her face.

Kirk did the talking. 'You're way behind,' he said. 'News should travel faster than that. I'm the new manager of the Two Spot. I'll be the proprietor soon.'

I looked at Cora again, bewildered. 'You want this guy thrown out?' I demanded.

Kirk grinned with smug confidence. 'I wouldn't try that, fella,' he said. 'There's a law against assault and battery. And the law's on my side.' Then looked at Cora. He said in a domineering kinda tone, 'I'm getting rid of that ham magician tonight. You'd better book another act to take his place tomorrow night. Understand?'

She nodded meekly. 'Yes, Lew. I'll do that.'

'Sorry I can't stop,' he said mockingly. 'I've got business to attend to. I'll leave you to continue your little chat with Cora.'

I stared after him as he walked along the corridor and closed the apartment door behind him.

Then I turned and stared at Cora. She was sitting with her head resting against the back of the chair and her eyes closed.

'What's that fella talking about?'

She opened her eyes and stared at me. 'What he says is true. He's the new manager.'

I just didn't know what to say. It was all so crazy. 'But, Ben,' I protested. 'Ben's your friend!'

'Why don't you leave me alone,' she said wearily.

I went over to her, grabbed her by the shoulder and shook her vigorously. 'You've gotta talk, Cora,' I said. 'What's this all about?'

She squirmed beneath my hand, and a look of horror came over her face. I let go of her like she was red hot and stepped back a coupla paces. 'I'm sorry,' I said bitterly. 'I forgot my touch hurt you that way.'

'But it doesn't, Hank,' she protested. Then she suddenly stopped short. 'I want you to believe me, Hank,' she said quietly. 'You misunderstood, that last time. It was because I wanted you. You had that effect on me!'

For a moment I stood there stupefied, and then it burst over me like a ray of light. That arm-biting act was because she was so emotionally worked up. It wasn't because she hated my touch, it was because she wanted me so badly that ...

'Cora,' I said. Impulsively I stepped toward her, and instinctively she flinched away from me.

'Don't touch me,' she pleaded. 'Don't touch me.'

My head was in a whirl. 'What goes on?' I demanded. 'What is this?'

She gave me a long, hard look. 'All right, Hank,' she said quietly. 'I'll have to tell you. I didn't want to tell you. But I can't let you leave here thinking I can't bear you to touch me.'

'It had better be good,' I said, breathing hard.

'Get yourself a drink and sit down,' she said.

'It happened a long while ago,' she began. 'So long ago it seems like a dream now. A bad dream. My mother died in childbirth. There was only my father, and when he too died, I was alone, miserable and just a little afraid. I suppose getting married was the obvious thing, and it wasn't long after my father died before I received a proposal.'

'How old were you?'

'Nearly 18,' she said.

'What kinda fella was he?'

She looked at me solemnly, and the blue shadows around her eyes were stronger. She became somehow pitiful and tragic. 'You know him,' she said. 'Lew Kirk. The trouble was, I didn't know him. I was young enough to be thrilled and excited. I can hardly believe now that I was so terribly happy the day we got married.'

As soon as she had started talking about getting married I had sensed what she was going to say. I remembered the recognition in her eyes when she'd seen Lew Kirk after he had tried to blackmail Virginia.

Cora went on slowly. 'Lew had a simple aim. Shortly after I became his wife he transferred all the property my father had left me to his name. I was young and innocent. I'd heard lots of stories about wives respecting their husbands. I respected my husband. I did what he asked without question. Foolishly I signed away everything I owned. I hadn't even a dress allowance. I relied upon Lew for every dime I got.'

'What was his business at the time?'

'Lawyer,' she said. 'He was in partnership with his brother Arthur, even then.'

'Your father was his client?'

'Naturally,' she said bitterly. 'He knew what I was worth to the dollar. That's why he married me.'

'What happened? Divorce?'

'Nothing so simple as that,' she said sadly. Then she looked up at me directly. 'You must have found me a strange woman, Hank.'

'In what way?'

A wisp of a smile crossed her lips. 'Well … I haven't exactly had hot pants, have I?'

'We don't have the same emotions.'

'There was a reason for it, in my case.' Her eyes looked into the past. She was reliving memories. She shuddered slightly. 'I was like most other girls, Hank, I guess. I was young, excitable and wanting to be loved. Lew knocked all that out of me.' She clenched her hands so tightly together that the knuckles stood out whitely. 'He was a beast, a fiend. He wasn't human. He didn't treat me as a wife. He did things that were beastly, unbearable.'

She was reliving her experiences. The humiliation and disgust she had felt then was somehow getting across to me. That showed just how strongly she felt about it.

'It did things to me, Hank,' she said. 'It seemed to dry me up. And after I left him, things didn't change. I couldn't feel the way I used to feel. Men didn't mean anything to me any longer. I'd lost something. Something inside me had been killed. I'd lost the ability to respond, and what made it worse was that I knew I was attractive to men.' Her eyes looked directly at me again. 'It was that way, Hank, the first time with you. The time I showed you. I just couldn't feel anything.'

I choked back something that was rising in my throat. 'It does happen. That kinda thing,' I said.

Her eyes looked into the past again. 'I stood it as long as I could. And then I left him. I hadn't any money and nowhere to go. But I was desperate. I made my plans slowly, and one day when he was out of town on business I took his cheque book, forged his signature, and drew fifty thousand dollars from his account.'

I whistled softly.

'I know,' she said. 'That was a lotta money. But it wasn't more than a quarter of the money I'd made over to him. The bank was hesitant about paying. But they knew I was his wife and they knew my securities were in his name. There was no way they could get in touch with him, and reluctantly they paid out.'

'I guess you had every right, at that.'

'Morally, yes,' she said. 'But legally, no. Forgery is a criminal offence, anywhere, anytime. But I was willing to take the risk. I left Mississippi and went to Los Angeles. I got lodgings and a job. I lived quietly for a coupla years, all the time afraid that the police or Lew would find me. And then, as time went on and I heard nothing of Lew, it began to dawn on me that probably he thought he'd got rid of me cheaply. I'd become a city girl by that time, you must remember. I was learning more about life, and I still had that fifty grand in the bank. It was there doing nothing. I was introduced to Ben Hilton at a party. He was a nice guy. I liked him. And after he'd got used to the idea that I had as much sexual impulse as a jellyfish, and still liked me enough to take me out, I got around to the idea of starting up in business with him.'

'Keep on talking,' I said. 'I'm hating Lew more and more every minute. I wanna hate him all I can before I start working on him. I wanna make a good job of it.'

She sighed wearily. 'There's nothing you can do,' she said. 'Together, Ben and I developed the business. But I never let it go out of my hands. I'd learned to hang on to things. I made Ben my manager and paid him well.

'He was satisfied, I guess. And then, after three years, we came to Chicago and started the Two Spot. You know what a success that has been.'

'And then I threw a spanner in the works by bringing along Virginia,' I said. 'Lew came after her – he saw you – recognised you – and began to put on the pressure?'

'Don't feel so bitter about it, Hank. It could have happened anytime.'

'You mustn't give way to him, Cora,' I said. 'You've gotta fight back. Life just isn't gonna be worthwhile otherwise. You leave Lew Kirk to me. I'll handle him.'

'I wish it were that easy,' she said bitterly. 'You see, Hank, everything's changed since he arrived. First there was you.' She gulped. 'That day when …' Her voice broke off. She held up her arm, which still wore sticking plaster, in explanation. 'I came alive that day. Something happened to me then that hadn't happened for years. I felt myself responding.'

'All wounds heal in time,' I said gently. 'The wounds of the body and the wounds of the mind.'

'But I'm dead again now, Hank. I'm all dried up inside. It was when he came back that it happened.'

'This won't take long,' I said. 'He'll be out on his ear.'

'It's not only that,' she said. 'That cheque. I forged it. He still has the cheque. That's what he's holding over me. Anytime he wants, he can take that to the police.'

'Let him take it,' I said. 'We'll fight the case. We'll prove the money was really yours, that it should never have been transferred to him.'

'I checked with my lawyers,' she said dully. 'I had my remedy. I've always had my remedy. I could always go to court and challenge the legality of a young girl of 18 passing her property to her husband. Maybe I'd win, maybe I'd lose. But obtaining that fifty grand was deliberate forgery. I just couldn't plead anything but guilty.' Her eyes were big as she looked at me. 'I couldn't face it, Hank,' she said. 'Ten years in jail, or even five years. I just couldn't face it. Everything I've built up would be lost by the time I came out. I'd have to start all over again, with nothing. I just couldn't face it.'

'What's the alternative?' I demanded. 'Kirk stepping in. He's taken over the managership of the Two Spot. He says he's going to take over the proprietorship. What's in it for you, anyway?'

'Liberty,' she said quietly. 'I can still run away again. This time he's covered all the angles. I won't have any money to take with me. But at least I'll have my liberty.'

I leaned forward and took her hands. For a moment her cool hands remained in mine, and then quickly she drew them from me. Her cheeks flushed. 'I'm sorry, Hank,' she said softly. 'He's made me feel that way.'

'You've got to do something,' I said. 'You just can't let it go on happening.'

'You suggest something,' she said wearily. 'I'll do it. I've worried myself sick figuring out something to do. I don't get no place.'

It still hurt the way she flinched from me. I swallowed hard. 'This is a delicate question to ask, Cora,' I said, breathing hard, 'but is this guy insisting on using you as a wife?'

Her eyes dulled with horror at the suggestion. 'No,' she whispered. 'But it couldn't hurt me worse if he had.'

'What d'ya mean?'

'Virginia,' she said quietly. 'He's got some hold over Virginia, too.'

I got up slowly. 'If he's touched that dame after all she's been through ...'

'I don't know what's happening,' she said. She seemed pitiful and forlorn. 'I know he shares Virginia's apartment and Virginia hasn't left her room since the day he arrived.'

'That does it,' I said, grimly. 'Lew Kirk really is gonna find himself trouble now.'

I strode across to the door. I was almost there when Cora said quietly: 'Just a moment.'

I half turned. She was sitting there with her eyes fixed on me imploringly.

'Believe me, Hank,' she said, with a break in her voice. 'I don't want anything to happen to Virginia. But don't do anything rash. He can send me to prison. Maybe he's got something like that on Virginia, too.'

I looked at her for a long while. I didn't say anything. Then I went out, closing the door softly behind me. It took all my willpower not to slam it. But her words were slowing me up. She was right. I ought to think this over. Acting hastily might cause trouble all round.

What I needed was a drink to help me mull the problem over in my mind.

I went downstairs and out into the street. I went straight across the road to a bar, and it wasn't altogether surprising that I should find Ben Hilton there, miraculously sobered, with his elbow crooked, sipping the inevitable whisky.

12

Ben Hilton put down his empty glass, signalled for a refill and looked at me steadily with wide blue eyes that seemed a million miles away.

'Well, what are you going to do?' he demanded.

I'd told Ben everything I'd learned, and indirectly invited his comments.

'That's just it,' I said. 'What am I going to do? Kirk's a lawyer. He knows the law. Any time we cause him trouble he can put Cora in jail. And maybe he's got something on Virginia.'

'What are you going to do?' repeated Ben.

I scratched my head. 'I dunno,' I said. 'I feel like wildcatting that guy, tearing him to pieces. But maybe that won't get us anywhere.'

'You ain't going to do nothing, then?' said Ben.

'I'll figure out something,' I said. 'Just leave it a while.'

Ben said slowly: 'All the time I've been here, I've been watching across the road. He ain't come back yet. But he's gonna come back sometime. And when he does ...' Ben paused, picked up his glass, which had been refilled, drank half of it, and smacked his lips appreciatively.

'And when he does?' I prompted.

'... I'm gonna go right over there and kill him,' said Ben softly.

I stared at him. 'You're joking,' I said. But I wasn't too sure

136

of it.

He opened his coat, fumbled in his inside breast pocket, and just for a moment showed me the butt of an automatic. Then he rebuttoned his coat. 'I ain't joking,' he said seriously. 'There's just one way to settle that guy. Kill him. Once he's out of the way, Cora won't have any worries.'

I cast a hasty look around the bar. Nobody could overhear us. I said urgently: 'You crazy dope. That wouldn't solve anything. You'd buy yourself a ticket to the hot-squat.'

He gave a funny kinda smile. 'I guess even then I'd be doing something useful. The way it is now, there'll be nothing but trouble for Cora. My way, it'd get rid of all her troubles.'

I stared at him with a new respect. I knew the guy went for Cora. But I guess it ain't often you bump up against a guy who's willing to die for the dame he loves. 'I like you for it, Ben,' I said. 'But I ain't gonna let you do it.'

His eyes were looking over my shoulder, through the window and across the street. He got up slowly. 'I hope you ain't gonna try and stop me, Janson,' he said. 'Because I'm gonna do it right now. Lew Kirk has just got back.'

I got up too, quick. 'Let's talk this over a bit more, Ben,' I urged.

'I ain't in a talking mood.' He circled around me and walked over to the door. I was undecided for a moment. I could call a cop, I could tackle him myself. But that wouldn't do any good. Maybe it would be a time-saver, get Ben taken down the jail for enquiry. But the chances were he had a licence to carry that gun. And then he'd shoot Kirk some other time. Sometime when I wasn't around.

I went after him. I linked my arm in his and said: 'You ain't gonna do this alone, Ben. I'm coming with you.'

'You'd better keep out of it,' he warned. 'They might make you an accessory. You can get the chair for that as well.'

I was thinking quickly. This looked like it was gonna be a showdown, with or without me. Maybe that was what was needed. But maybe it could be handled differently.

'You're running your head into trouble unnecessarily, Ben,' I said. 'All we wanna do is to protect Cora. But you don't want to kill Kirk to do that.'

He didn't answer. His mouth just quirked in a strained grin.

'All we want from him is that forged cheque,' I said. 'If we're gonna take the law into our own hands, we don't have to kill the guy. We can just rough him up till we get what we want.'

We'd crossed the road by this time and got around back of the Two Spot. We started up the stairs to the corridor where Kirk had his apartment.

'Do what I say, Ben,' I pleaded. 'Don't start shooting. Let's avoid that if we can.'

'Fellas like that don't deserve to live,' he said bitterly. 'The world's a lot better without them.'

I made one, last desperate attempt. 'Killing Kirk might not be the answer,' I said. 'He's got that forged cheque around somewhere. How d'you know he hasn't arranged to have it posted to the police if he winds up dead anytime?'

That hit home. Ben hesitated momentarily in his steps. As we walked along the corridor toward Kirk's door I could see him turning it over in his mind. Just before he pushed the bell-button, he said: 'You may have something there, fella. What was that you said about roughing him up a little?'

'We'll do it between us,' I said. 'This guy's earned everything he's got coming to him.'

By the time Kirk got the door open, Ben had levelled the automatic. Kirk stared down at the shiny barrel pointing directly at his belly and gave an uneasy smile.

'Back up,' said Ben grimly.

Kirk backed up and we followed him in. I shut the door behind me.

'Put that thing away,' said Kirk. 'I don't want trouble, and if you put it away I'll forget everything.'

Ben stepped in close and ran his fingers over Kirk's pockets. Apparently he wasn't armed. Ben dropped his automatic into his pocket and smiled grimly. For the first time, I realised that the pleasant Ben Hilton could become a tough customer when he wanted.

'Now get out,' said Kirk as though he had secured a victory. 'Get out and I'll forget this. Otherwise I'll call the cops ...'

For a guy who was permanently fifty percent lush, Ben's judgment was good. His arm travelled in a short arc and his knuckles smacked against Kirk's jaw with a meaty noise. As Kirk sprawled on the floor, trying to get his breath and spitting blood, Ben slowly and deliberately unbuttoned his jacket, tossed it to one side and rolled up his sleeves.

Kirk levered himself up on one arm and glared at Ben balefully. But there was apprehension in his eyes, too. He made no attempt to get to his feet.

'Get up,' said Ben.

'You'll get sent down for this,' snarled Kirk. 'I'll make you pay.'

Ben booted him in the ribs. Not hard, but enough to make Kirk yell. Kirk rolled over, hugging his side, and then with a surprising speed erupted into action. He kinda ran along on his knees, climbing to his feet at the same time. He went running down the corridor toward the living-room. Ben was right behind him and got his shoulder against the door before Kirk could close it. As soon as I got my shoulder to the door as well, Kirk couldn't hold it closed.

It didn't last long. I'd have liked to have taken a hand myself, the way I felt about Kirk. But I reckoned Ben had first place.

It took about ten minutes. At the end of that time the room was a shambles, and Ben had propped Kirk up in a chair, half-conscious, his face, nose and mouth bleeding and his breath rasping in his throat as though he had sandpaper for lung-tissue.

'That's just to start with,' said Ben. He licked his bleeding knuckles. 'Now we're gonna get somewhere. Where d'ya keep that forged cheque?'

Kirk looked at him apprehensively. 'I don't know what you're talking about,' he said.

Ben slapped his face hard. The apartment bell rang at the same time.

'See who it is,' rapped Ben. 'Scare them away.'

I went along the corridor to the front door and opened up. It was Cora. She was wearing a simple blue frock. Her eyes were worried and her face unnaturally pale. 'What's happening, Hank?' she asked anxiously. 'There was such a noise next door.'

'It's a party,' I said. 'You can join in.'

When we got back to the living-room, Ben had knocked Kirk cold and was just finishing tying his ankles together. He'd already tied Kirk's hands behind his back.

'Just sloosh some water over him,' said Ben.

I went for the water jug. Cora said anxiously: 'Ben! What are you doing?'

'Keep out of this, Cora,' he said grimly. 'We're getting things settled.'

I shot the water straight into Kirk's face. It brought him around. He blinked his eyes and then looked around. When Ben moved toward him he flinched away. Ben grinned. 'Now. How about that forged cheque?'

Kirk's eyes flicked from Ben to Cora and then back to Ben. 'There ain't no forged cheque,' he protested.

'Is he a liar, Cora?' asked Ben.

Cora gave me a reproving look. 'You shouldn't have told Ben,' she said.

'We're all human,' I told her. 'He understands the way it is.'

'Well?' demanded Ben.

'He's holding it over my head,' admitted Cora.

Ben slowly got out his cigarette lighter. 'You'd better hold him down, Hank.' he said.

I got around behind Kirk and crooked my arm around his neck. I was half-choking him. After what he had done to Cora, it was all I could do to prevent myself from choking him fully. Ben stooped down. I couldn't see what he was doing properly but I could guess. Cora screamed and Kirk gave such a pained squirm that I almost lost him. He even managed to yell, too, although I was half-choking him.

Ben was breathing hard. 'Well, Kirk,' he said. 'What about it? Or do you want me to do it proper? That was just your calf.

How would you like it if I take off your shoe and sock and burn your leg off up to the knee?'

Kirk was moaning piteously. He kept repeating over and over again, 'Don't do it. Don't do it.'

'Hold him, Hank,' said Ben.

I wasn't liking this. But I liked even less the idea of Ben going to the hot-squat on account of Kirk. This time I braced myself for Kirk's leap of pain. And after that Kirk was sobbing, willing to do anything.

'Cut it out,' yelled Ben above Kirk's whining. 'Just tell me what I wanna know. Where's that forged cheque?'

'In the safe,' mouthed Kirk. 'In the other room.'

'Where's the key?'

'It's … a combination,' Kirk jerked out. His face was white and his lips blue. He was whistling with pain when he spoke.

'You'd better come and do it,' said Ben.

There was no fight left in Kirk. He'd do anything to avoid going through that again. We untied his legs and arms and dragged him across to the door of the bedroom. When we tried the door it was locked. 'The key,' Kirk said weakly. 'Over there.' He pointed to an earthenware decorative pot on the mantelpiece. The bedroom key was inside.

It wasn't strange that he had locked the bedroom door. It wasn't until we'd got the door open that I remembered Virginia. And Virginia was in the bedroom. And when I saw her, I got mad all over again. I could have torn Kirk apart with my own hands.

I'd thought that Cora was pale and hollow-eyed, but beside Virginia, Cora looked like a lusty country girl with the flush of health on her cheeks.

Virginia was sitting on the bed, pressing herself up against the wall, scared to death. Her face was a deathly white and her eyes were sunk far back, so that their green light seemed to shine with a wild brilliance deep down in black caverns. Her mouth kept twitching nervously, and every now and again one of her limbs jerked like it was attached to a string. She was wearing just her camiknickers.

I gulped. 'Virginia,' I said. I heard my voice break, and I made a step toward her. She recoiled from me, her face contorted in horror, and she screamed. It wasn't loud. A low, fluted scream. I turned around and looked at Kirk. I didn't say anything. But my face must have said everything. Ben stepped between us. He smacked his hand across my face. 'Hold it, Hank,' he yelled. 'Hold it, you damned fool. Wait till we get what we want.'

I was glad he did that. I think right then I might have killed Kirk with my bare hands. I got a grip on myself and relaxed. I felt the sweat standing out all over me. I took out my handkerchief and mopped my brow. 'Thanks, Ben,' I said. 'We'll deal with him later.'

'Don't let him touch me,' pleaded Kirk.

Ben shoved him roughly by the shoulder. 'The cheque,' he said. 'Give. The cheque.'

Kirk was shaking with fear now. He couldn't take his eyes off me. There was a white, panicky pallor to his face and his fat fingers trembled visibly as he pushed aside a picture and revealed a small wall-safe.

He opened it up, twiddled the combination dial and, still looking at me fearfully and shaking like a leaf, opened the safe door. He put his hand inside and pulled out a big envelope. He would have fumbled in the envelope except that Ben snatched it from him, tore it open and rustled through the contents.

'Is this it, Cora?' said Ben.

Cora took the cheque that Ben handed her. She looked at it. 'This is it,' she said quietly.

'Tear it up,' said Ben.

Slowly and deliberately Cora tore it into pieces. She kept on tearing like she'd never finish. She tore it into pieces so small it was like confetti.

'Flush it down the pan, Cora,' I said. 'Just to be on the safe side.' Then I turned my eyes toward Kirk. 'And now,' I said venomously. 'Now it's my turn.'

Kirk said desperately: 'You'd better not do it, Janson. This ain't the end. I can cause trouble. Lots of trouble. I'll make you wish you'd never started this.'

I moved in. I moved in slowly. I had all the time in the world.

Kirk moved quickly. He dived his hands into the wall safe. When he spun around I saw something shining in his hand. I didn't wait to see what it was. I aimed at his fat, pasty face and felt satisfaction as my fist cleaved his flesh. Kirk gave a surprised kinda grunt as he smashed back against the wall and the shiny object in his hand went flying across the room. From the corner of my eye I got a glimpse of Virginia leaping across the bed and diving for it. And then I was in again, my left burying itself up to the wrist in Kirk's belly and my right jarring against his jaw as his head jack-knifed downwards.

I stood back and watched Kirk as he lay slumped against the wall. 'Get up,' I said bitterly. 'I ain't started yet.'

'All right,' said Virginia, grimly. 'Stand well clear.' I glanced at her in surprise. She'd picked up the gun and was holding it in a shaking hand. She was pointing it at Kirk, but was looking at me and Ben. 'Get out of the way,' she said.

She wasn't herself. Anyone could see that. Her mouth was still twitching and there was something wrong with her eyes. They gleamed too brightly.

'Cut that out,' said Ben quickly.

'Yeah,' I said. 'Put that gun down, Virginia.' I moved forward toward her warily.

'Stand back,' she shrilled. 'I don't want to hurt you.'

'There ain't no need for that, Virginia,' I said.

I didn't say any more, because she squeezed off then. She triggered the gun three times, and the reports sounded on top of each other. Their repercussions intermingled, making one concussion against my eardrums.

I guess I was so surprised I must have stood there for several seconds. Then Virginia dropped the gun and collapsed on the bed, sobbing.

I didn't wanna look at Kirk. The gun had been pointing at him when it went off. But I had to do it. Maybe the gun had been unsteady in her hand: only two of those three bullets had hit him in the head. He hadn't even known he was dying. He'd been unconscious when the first bullet hit him.

Cora came bursting out from the bathroom when she heard the shots. She gave one look at Kirk and then began to scream her head off.

Ben grabbed her. He pulled her arms to her sides and gripped her tightly. 'Shuddup,' he warned.

She went on screaming.

'Shuddup,' roared Ben again.

That still didn't get him results.

He rammed her down in a chair, smacked her face hard from side to side, and when that didn't get results, he dashed into the kitchen and came back with a jug of water.

Emptying that over Cora did achieve results. Her screams changed to a startled gurgling.

But I wasn't paying much attention to this. I was looking at Virginia. She was lying on the bed, her shoulders shuddering convulsively as she sobbed like her heart would break. She was wearing only camiknickers. Her long slim thighs were splayed out shamelessly, so I couldn't avoid seeing them if I wanted.

But it wasn't her legs I was looking at so much. It was the ugly red punctures high up on her thigh near the groin.

And then, knowing what Kirk had done to her, I was glad that he was dead. And if Virginia hadn't killed him, I'd have done it myself.

13

Five minutes later it was so quiet in that room that you could have heard the clock ticking in the restaurant across the road. Ben had draped a blanket over Kirk. Cora was sitting and twisting a handkerchief to pieces in her hands, oblivious of her soaked frock. I'd got Virginia propped up with a coupla pillows behind her. She was breathing quietly now. The wild gleam had gone from her eyes and her body wasn't twitching so much.

Ben poked a cigarette in his mouth and struck a match. It rasped loudly in the silence of the room, and we watched closely as he applied it to the end of the cigarette, extinguished it, and tossed it into an ashtray.

'What do we do now?' he asked.

'How d'ya feel, kid?' I said to Virginia.

'Get it over,' she said wearily. 'Call the cops.'

'Virginia,' I pleaded. 'Why d'ya do it? It didn't have to be that way.'

Her voice was dull, toneless. 'He would have told anyway.'

'Told what?'

'I guess it's in the safe, too,' she said. 'Look for it, will you? It's a photograph.'

I looked at her strangely. Then I got up and went across to the safe. There were lots of envelopes and securities and other things. I found it at last. It was a strange kinda photograph. It showed a man lying on the floor with a gun in his hand. An obvious suicide. The photograph had been angled strangely.

The way it was angled showed a lady's handbag lying open on an occasional table. It was one of those handbags that bears the owner's initials. The initials caught my eye straight away. The initials were V L.

I looked at the photograph and then looked at Virginia. 'I don't know what the hell this is about,' I said. 'But we could have handled it for you. You didn't have to do it this way.'

'It's no good, Hank,' she said. 'You heard him. He was gonna tell anyway.'

'Tell what?'

'I killed Arthur Kirk,' she said quietly. Then she looked at my shocked face defiantly. 'I had to kill him. It was self-defence. He'd been asking me to marry him. I wouldn't have it. He got me to go to his house, saying it was business. There was nobody else in the house. Nobody could hear my screams.' She gave a long kinda sigh. 'He was big and strong. There was no other way of stopping him from getting what he wanted.'

'You killed him!' I said incredulously.

'I was struggling with him,' she went on, as though I hadn't interrupted. 'He kept his gun in his desk drawer. I got hold of it. I didn't mean to shoot him. I only meant to frighten him with it. But he grabbed my hand and tried to get the gun. Suddenly it went off, and then ...' Her voice broke off.

'Wait a minute,' I said. 'I can't take all this in. What about the photograph?'

She went on tiredly. 'It was some time before I realised that he was dead. I was frightened, terribly frightened. And then some part of my brain urged me to get out of there, say nothing about it. Just as I was going, I remembered the gun. I wiped off my fingerprints and put the gun into his hand. I wanted it to look like suicide.'

Cora said incredulously: 'You mean you killed Arthur Kirk?'

Virginia's green eyes stared at her. 'That's why I couldn't let them lynch the negro,' she said. 'I couldn't let him suffer for what I'd done. I had to save him from that.'

I scratched my head. 'The photograph,' I said. 'I don't get it.'

'I didn't sleep that night, and suddenly I remembered my

handbag. I'd left it there. I'd left it in that house. I'd left it there with the dead man.'

'They didn't say anything about it at the trial.'

'They didn't know about it. I went back the same night to get it. I was scared out of my life every inch of the way. And when I got there, the bag had disappeared.'

I looked at the photograph again. The photograph told a definite story. The handbag had been there while the dead man lay on the floor.

'This photograph's a frame, then?'

She shook her head. 'The photograph's genuine. Lew Kirk must have returned immediately after Arthur was killed. He must have realised I'd killed Arthur and tried to make it look like suicide. He took that photograph. A few days after the finding of the body, he called on me personally and gave me a parcel. When I unwrapped the parcel … the handbag was inside. He hadn't said anything. But I knew and he knew.'

Cora said pleadingly: 'But why did you shoot him? You didn't have to do that. It was …'

'I know,' said Virginia quietly. 'I'll go to the chair now. But it couldn't go on. Being under his thumb was worse than being dead. He's been here with me five days now. Five days of hell.' She held out her hands in front of us so we could see how they were twitching. 'I'd rather die,' she said simply.

'You poor kid,' said Cora. 'I know what he can be like.'

'We've gotta get out of this,' I said. 'There must be some legal excuse for shooting a louse.'

'I don't care now,' said Virginia. 'It's all over. I don't care what happens.' She looked up, and somehow her face seemed to lose its pallor and the dark rings around her eyes and regain some of its radiance. 'You've been real nice to me, Hank,' she said. 'Thanks a lot.'

I was all screwed up inside. My voice was more of a sob than anything, I guess. After all she had been through, after all she had suffered, to finish this way! 'Virginia,' I gulped. 'You've gotta make a break for it, kid. We'll help you. We can cover up for you.'

She shook her head decisively. 'No more running away, Hank,' she said. 'I'm going to face it this time. I made my choice. You can't beat anything by running from it.'

I looked at Ben. He looked away quickly, trying not to meet my eyes. I looked at Cora. She was looking at me pleadingly. 'There must be something!' she murmured.

'There's the phone,' said Virginia, nodding. 'Be a good fella. Get the cops, will ya, Hank?'

'Give it a little time,' I urged. 'We can cover up somehow.'

'If you won't do it, I will,' said Virginia. She swung her legs like she was gonna get up. As she moved, the edge of her camiknickers rode up over her flank, exposing once more those horrible red punctures in her skin.

'Just a minute, Virginia,' I said. There must have been something in my voice that made her stop. 'Did Kirk do those?' I pointed.

Her face set and her eyes blazed. She held out her hands again and watched them twitch. 'He's been doping me. Small two-hourly injections. Working up to bigger doses. Said he was going to get me so full of dope I'd do anything he asked in order to get more. He told me he was going to make me work up such a craving that I'd do anything he wanted to satisfy it. Literally anything!' She shuddered.

I counted the blotches on her legs. There were about twenty. 'Listen to me, Virginia,' I said excitedly. 'I'm getting ideas. Are there any more punctures?'

She looked at me steadily for a moment. 'It's important?'

'Very,' I said seriously. She pulled shoulder straps down over her arms and cupped one breast in her hand so she could lift it. Tender skin immediately below the swell of her breast was reddened and punctured in a score or more places. I clucked my tongue. The more I saw of Kirk's handiwork, the more I figured he was a good guy to be dead.

'Where did he keep it?' I demanded.

Virginia nodded across the room toward a wardrobe. The drawer was locked. Ben had to break it open. He brought it across to me. It was in a neat leather case, a hypodermic complete with six capsules of liquid.

'Listen to me carefully, Virginia,' I said. 'We're gonna tell the police. Sure, you're gonna take the stand. But you knew that was coming anyway. But we're gonna beat the rap. There'll be extenuating circumstances.'

Her green eyes stared at me. 'I killed him,' she said simply. 'That's all there is to it.'

'But there were special circumstances,' I pointed out. 'You didn't know what you were doing. You were a hop-head. You were stuffed so full of dope you didn't know you were doing it. Understand?'

Cora said quickly: 'You've got to do it, honey. You've got to do it.'

I looked at Ben. 'I guess Hank's right,' he said. 'There ain't no point in getting tried on account of that skunk.'

Deep down in Virginia's green eyes I saw the light of hope dawn. 'You mean I might get away with it, Hank?'

'You've got to play it straight, kid. You'll beat the death sentence for sure. But what's more, maybe you'll get off and be sent to a sanatorium. They'll work on you to get you cured. After that, probably a parole.'

The hope dwindled in her eyes. 'There's just one thing wrong,' she said. 'I'm not a hop-head.'

I looked at the hypodermic. I looked at the capsules and I looked at Virginia. 'You can be,' I said grimly. 'It'll mean taking a pretty hard shot. Maybe you'll be ill, very ill, for a long time. It's a chance you've gotta decide for yourself.'

'You mean,' she faltered, looking at the hypodermic.

'That's it,' I said. 'We'll stuff you to the eyebrows. Kirk was building you up slowly. You'll have to take it all in one jolt. You may even crack up. But it's a decision you've got to make. What do you say, kid?'

'What can I say?' she said faintly. 'I've got no choice, if it means a new start.'

We hadn't much time to waste. Blood congeals quickly. I didn't want nosey cops asking questions about what was happening between the time we heard the shooting and the time we phoned them.

I pricked the capsule, squeezed its contents into the hypodermic and got my thumb on the plunger. Virginia rolled over on her side and I puckered up her flesh between my fingers, slid the point beneath the skin and pressed home the plunger. Virginia gave a sharp intake of breath, but that was all.

'It'll work out all right, kid,' I said cheerfully, as I broke the second capsule.

'You help, Hank,' she said softly. 'It always helps having you around. I guess ...' Her voice broke off momentarily as the needle slid under her skin again. Then she went on: 'I guess you're a nice kinda guy to have around.'

'I guess a fella could consider himself lucky having you around,' I retorted.

'When it's all over, Hank,' she said. Then she winced as the needle slid in for the third time. This time she gritted her teeth as I pressed on the plunger, slowly sending the dope flooding into her system.

'What were you saying?'

'When it's all over, Hank,' she began again. Then she pulled a face and suddenly arched her back. The corners of her mouth drooped and her eyes seemed to melt. I kept on pressing the plunger until the hypodermic was empty. I withdrew the needle and filled the hypodermic for the last time. I looked at Ben.

'Think she can take it?'

'She's got to,' he said. 'She's gotta be hopped up when the police arrive, so she's crazy for it.'

I wiped the sweat off her brow, and from a long way away she tried to smile at me. 'When it's all over, Hank,' she said weakly, 'you'll be around, won't you?'

'Sure,' I said. 'Sure.' I slid the needle in under her skin, and the pain came out from between her teeth. Her fingers, strangely claw-like, groped out and fastened on my forearm. I kept pressing home the plunger, and her fingers gouged with incredible strength. I could feel my arm being bruised. And then the plunger went right home.

'Put this back in the drawer,' I said, giving Ben the hypodermic. I bent over Virginia. The breath was rasping in her throat, and her eyes were closed. I opened one eye and gazed at her pupil. It was shrunken to a pinpoint. I pulled back a tendril of hair from her forehead, and remembered how she had said: 'When it's all over, Hank, you'll be around, won't you?' I remembered what a tough time she'd had, and I remembered other things, too. I leaned over and gently kissed her on the lips. She made no response. She was loaded with that stuff. They'd have to work weeks on her to get her back to normal.

I turned around, and Cora was watching me with those calm eyes of hers.

'I feel kinda sorry for her,' I explained.

'She had her head screwed on right,' said Cora. 'If she'd tried sticking it out the way I did, she'd have ended up dried up inside too.'

I walked to the telephone and picked it up. When they got me through to the right department, I said wearily: 'I'm speaking from an apartment above the Two Spot. A hop-head has just gone out of her mind. She's shot up a guy. You'd better send some fellas over.'

'Want an ambulance?'

'Just a blood-wagon,' I said. 'The guy's cold. Sure, I'll wait here till you arrive.'

I hung up, turned around and looked at Virginia. Her eyes were closed and her face was white and troubled. She was moaning now and her body writhed uncontrollably as she endured maddening, horrible nightmares. It wasn't pleasant to see her looking that way.

'You'd better get back to your room, Cora,' Ben said. 'We'll handle this.'

'What do I tell the police?'

I said: 'We heard the shots from your apartment and when we came round there was Kirk lying dead on the floor. The dame was unconscious.'

'Will she tell the same story?' asked Cora.

'What does it matter what she says?' I replied. 'What she

says won't make sense. She's a hop-head. Remember?'

Cora got up. She kept her eyes away from Virginia, who was tossing and moaning. 'I guess maybe I had better wait next door,' she said. She was looking all-in.

'That's the idea,' I said. I looked at Ben. 'Maybe you'd better make sure she gets there safely.'

'Yeah, I guess I'll do that,' he said.

By the time he got back, Virginia had rolled off the bed twice and scratched my face to pieces as I grappled with her. She was making ugly animal noises, clawing at the bedspread and slavering.

Seeing her like that got me sweating all over.

Ben gave me a keen look. 'You look like you could do with a drink, brother.'

'Sure,' I said. 'I could do with a drink.' Then I winced as Virginia gave a low drawn-out animal growl. I knew I was going to go on hearing that in my sleep for nights to come.

'Get yourself a drink, Hank,' he said. 'I'll stay here with her.'

I got as far as the bedroom door. I could hear the police sirens outside, and I could see the whisky decanter over on the sideboard. I said softly: 'There's just one thing, Ben.'

'What's that?'

'Cora,' I said. 'I reckon you must be aces high with her. Maybe she's frigid now. But she'll get over that shock in time. Just hang on, fella. Just hang on. She'll get better.'

'You don't have to tell me,' he said. 'I'm hanging on just as long as she'll let me.'

Virginia started making that horrible animal noise again. Only much more loudly this time. Sweat was running down from my forehead like I was in a Turkish bath. Yet there were icy shudders running down my spine. I took a grip on myself, clenched my hands tightly and walked down the passage toward the door. I could hear heavy boots outside, and the doorbell was ringing like it would never stop.

'When it's all over, Hank,' she'd said, 'you'll still be around, won't you?'

There was something pricking at the back of my eyes. I let

them worry the bell while I took time off to mop my brow. Then I dabbed the handkerchief against the corners of my eyes, blinked a coupla times, and opened the door. I jerked my thumb over my shoulder. 'Right through,' I said huskily.

Other Crime Titles available from Telos Publishing